THE NINE TIGER MAN

Reviews

JOHN BARKHAM, NEW YORK WORLD A delicious tale of low behaviour in high places; with particular attention to the activities of an irresistible and gifted East Indian Prince who takes his own form of revenge against the entire English Empire by inducting a bevy of highborn English females into the fine points of Oriental eroticism, proving that Debrett's Peerage is no match at all for the Karma Sutra . . .

REBECCA WEST This book is exquisite — and a *new* story.

TERENCE RATTIGAN, (scriptwriter for George Cukor's unfinished feature film, 20th Century Fox) Romantic, outrageous, savage and comic . . . It is the purest ironic comedy, almost, let's face it, black.

OBSERVER An outrageous nineteenth-century romance . . . the languishing Lady Florence and her down-to-earth maid fall enjoyable prey to the lusts of a Maharaja's favourite during the Sepoy Mutiny . . . a mocking confrontation of the attitudes of *Clarissa* and *Fanny Hill* set against an exotically sensuous Indian background.

DAILY MAIL Cynical, sensual, amusing.

RALPH BLUM, VOGUE Lesley Blanch's first novel is a smasher.

Lesley Blanch

THE NINE TIGER MAN

A Satirical Romance

BookBlast ePublishing, London

To
Nancy Mitford
who wrote of love in a cold climate,
this tale of love in a warm climate
is dedicated with affection.

I

The swing was made of silver, its seat carved in the form of a crouching tiger. Its ropes were made of twisted silver chains, and the hooks were serpents' heads. A little pagoda-like umbrella, also of silver, with pearl and coral tassels, was suspended above the seat. It had been made for some Maharaja's favourite, a Rani or a dancing girl, to hang on the rooftop of a marble palace where the rival beauties of the zenana enticed their lord and master with curious antics, twining themselves round him or each other or the swing, while in the surrounding jungles parakeets were clustered in the treetops like green fruits, and the leopards and the tigers prowled below.

Now the swing dangled forlornly from an iron girder supporting the Gothic-revival conservatory at Bogwood, an English country house belonging to the Dowager Viscountess Boxhampton. It had been presented to her that day by the Rao Jagnabad, her Hindu protégé, a Rajput chieftain of surpassing good looks and wealth who had joined the Bogwood house party as guest of honour, arriving by the London train with some rum-looking luggage, as Stokes the coachman said, helping the porters strap the swing, wrapped in an Afghan carpet, on the roof of the carriage.

'A real toff, even if he don't wear boots,' was the verdict of Henry, the second footman, who had been unpacking for those gentlemen who came without their own valets, and the Rao was such, surprisingly for an Eastern potentate. No one could deny the magnificence of his dress, but as Henry said, yellow slippers were not at all the same thing as handmade boots.

'Still, a swell if ever I saw one,' he added. Even Mr Brill the butler let this pass unchallenged; though grudgingly, for no one outside Burke's Peerage had any reality for him. Looking eastwards, he could not admit of breeding beyond Vienna. The marble halls of the Great Mogul, had he been aware of them, would have been but gipsy encampments.

The conservatory was in darkness, but light from the dining room beyond filtered through so that the silver swing glowed as if incandescent. Outside, shivering in the damp night air, Rosie was gaping through the glass at this fabulous object. Peering closer, through the potted palms, the maidenhair ferns and the bold silhouette of the gloxinias, she had a very good view of the dinner party too.

Rosie was in service at Bogwood Hall, working in the still room, or the sewing room, or running errands, but lately had been promoted to wait on Miss Florence, the Dowager's only daughter. A few minutes before she had slipped out of the kitchen unperceived, for the hierarchy of the domestic staff, headed by Mr Brill and seconded by Mrs Maggot the cook, moving with sacerdotal gravity, were presenting the classic, if massive, menu of that time: turtle soup, tench stewed in wine, Scotch salmon, haunch of mutton, partridges, roast duckling, Nesselrode pudding and all the wines and elegant trimmings such a menu imposed. Rosie had seized on a lull between the Nesselrode pudding and the dessert to absent herself. She wanted to see the silver swing and the grand guests, for there had been much talk about them in the servants' hall. Now, on this raw night late in October 1856, she was standing on tiptoe, her thin shoes squelching in a muddy flower -bed, her upturned nose flattened against the glass.

Between the silver-gilt épergnes and trails of stephanotis which decorated the dinner table Rosie could watch all the grand folk who had come down from London. The house party numbered eighteen, not counting the local gentry who had been bidden to dine. She could distinguish each one easily enough from the descriptions with which William, the first footman and a wag, had regaled the servants' hall. Now she picked out the Cabinet Minister and his pinch-faced wife, feathers nodding; the Lord-Lieutenant of the county, a foreign Ambassador and his lady ('Eye-ties or Frogs,' said William, who saw no difference), and the old Duke whose estates marched with those of the Dowager. He was shouting across his neighbour, an opulent lady, wife of the Lord Mayor of London, and addressing himself to Mr Edward Mulgrove, Miss Florence's fiancé, who did not look best pleased, for he had been whispering attentively in Florence's ear and clearly wished to continue doing so. The old Duke's stables were said to be the best in England, the coachman had told Rosie, so no doubt he was shouting about horses, she thought, watching his mouth open and shut clownishly, while no sound reached her through the glass. Across the table was the beautiful widow who had buried five husbands, according to William. A beauty in her own way, or anyhow in the way of five husbands, Rosie conceded, she was now seated between a bottle-nosed admiral and a one-armed military gentleman, (perhaps already marked down as the sixth?). 'Bigwigs, every one of them,' said Mr Brill, who dearly loved the nobility and gentry. But Rosie's bright green eyes had ranged them all, only to return again to the guest of honour seated at the Dowager's right hand.

His strange, fierce face with its heavy dark eyebrows meeting in an unbroken sweep below a round scarlet mark painted in the middle of his brow was like nothing she had ever seen or imagined. He wore a necklace of enormous pearls – seven rows of magnificence – and from the centre hung rubies the size of the plums Rosie had been making into jam that very morning. The buttons of his violet-and-gold brocaded coat were clusters of diamonds; and there were more of them in his ears. They sparked fire as he moved his turbaned head with a curiously restive movement, which reminded her of the hunters she sometimes saw being led round the stable yard by that bandy-legged little groom who eyed her so saucily.

But then, one way or another, all men eyed Rosie. She was

going on twenty, pretty, pert and lusty. She had come out of an orphanage under the patronage of the Dowager, to enter her service a few years earlier. Polethorpe, the Dowager's vinegary maid, had set about training her. Between her duties in the still room and mending the household linen under the supervision of the sewing-maid, Rosie told William she couldn't call her soul her own. But now that Miss Florence was 'out' and requiring more attention than Polethorpe could spare her, Rosie was promoted, spending her time between the pickles and preserves of the still room, and the hairbrushes, stay-laces and lotions in Miss Florence's room, listening to her rattling on about the novels she read in such quantities. Now Rosie was one of the upstairs staff, the kitchen said she gave herself airs. 'Who does she think she is?' asked Charlie the gardener's boy indignantly – he'd brought the vegetables round to the kitchen door and had hoped to corner and kiss her, but had been slapped for his pains. Rosie didn't care much who she was; she knew exactly what she was a very pretty girl. Her exuberant flesh strained against the starched print of her bodice and quite weakened the lofty resolves of Mr George, the Dowager's youngest son, now home on leave from his regimental duties in India, while the far less lofty resolves of both William and Henry, as well as of Stubbs the pimply pageboy, were only kept in check by Mr Brill, who was himself not above pinching Rosie's plump rump when he found her alone in the still room.

But Rosie had not come out of an orphanage for nothing. She'd learned how to get along with men. There had been countless escapades with village boys behind the haystack, even furtive meetings with a trustee of the orphanage, ever since she could remember – ever since, in fact, the Reverend had come and fetched her away from the labourer's cottage when her widower father had died clasping a struggling pig and an empty bottle of gin under the impression he was having a good time. She was just ten – it was in fact her birthday that very day, as she confided to the Reverend. He had become very affectionate.

'Quite a big girl now,' he said, 'quite big . . .' Rosie remembered how his pale, puffy hands had stroked her inquisitively. Before placing her in the orphanage he had taken her to the Vicarage, where he lived alone with his mother, but the old lady was away for a few days, visiting her married daughter, so the Reverend had taken care of Rosie himself, bringing her plum cake and even a glass of hot sherry wine after she'd gone to bed. 'Just as if you were my own little girl,' he'd said, and Rosie smiled grimly, remembering the inquisitive hands.

All that was a long while ago. Now she was nicely placed at the big house and could take her pick of admirers. She rather fancied Stokes, the coachman, and was playing him off against William. She watched William going round the table removing yet another set of plates, (the washing up was going to take all night, thought Rosie, what with Mr Brill being so particular about the different patterns not being mixed up),while Mr Brill himself moved majestically round refilling the wine glasses. Rosie noticed that the Indian gentleman always refused the wines and was returning the toasts in soda water. It's funny, she thought, to see all that jewellery on a man. Covered in it, he was, yet somehow, it seemed part of himself, like an animal's fur, or a bird's feathers, and not just hung on for a party like the stuff the Dowager, or Miss Florence, or any of the grand ladies wore. William had not made up a thing, the foreign gentleman looked the spit of Satan in those big Bible paintings that hung on the stairs.

There was indeed something daemonic in the dark, impassive face, the face of a hunter awaiting his prey, or perhaps Satan, biding his time for sinners. The nose was delicately shaped but rather flattened, the wide nostril flaring, the long, heavy-lidded black eyes slanted above high cheekbones, and the full lips were chiselled into a faint sneer and framed in a small, curiously shaped black beard. This was brushed upwards and outwards in the two aggressive thrusts, symbolic assertions of virility, which were the distinguishing mark of all Rajput warriors.

The Rao Jagnabad had arrived in London a few months earlier hoping to settle a territorial dispute raging between his adopted father, ruler of a small Rajput kingdom, and the inflexible Commissioners of the East India Company. He was trying to interest Her Majesty's Government in his case, and to that end had been much seen about London. His strange and brilliant appearance, as well as the grave attention with which he listened to the advice of his well wishers, endeared him to London Society. A number of ladies, both young and old, were said to find him irresistible, but the deference of his manner allayed even the most suspicious. The gentlemen too found him a capital fellow, as good a judge of horseflesh as the best, (by which they meant an Englishman), a great hunter 'a nine tiger man' it was said with respect, game for anything in the way of high stakes, and generous with an apparently inexhaustible supply of the finest cheroots imaginable. Still, it wouldn't do to let him get above himself – after all, he was an outsider. If he knew what was good for him he'd keep his distance.

The Queen herself was rumoured to be interested in his claims – but then Her Majesty was partial to everything and everybody pertaining to her Indian conquests. Only a few years earlier she had graciously deigned to accept the Koh-i-noor, the legendary 'Mountain of Light', from the hands of its former owner, the young Maharaja Dhuleep Singh, who had been deposed by her Government in 1849 and was now her protégé, a most gratifying convert to Christianity, his turbaned head often to be seen bowed in worship in the royal pew at Kew Green where he resided with his tutors. Soon Indian princes became the rage. They were the embodiment of those faraway kingdoms of the East which have always held a powerful sway over the British people, inflaming their imaginations while lining their pockets.

No wonder Florence was in such a taking, cold shouldering her fiancé and gozzling at the stranger. Rosie watched her young mistress and saw that her eyes were indeed fixed far too often on the Hindu and that she was blushing and paling by turns. Whatever was she about! If Mr Edward or her Ladyship were to notice! There had been talk already in the servants' hall. William had all the facts. Miss Florence had refused to walk round the home farm with Mr Edward after luncheon.

'Not she,' said William. 'She wanted to spend the afternoon in that fancy silver swing the foreign prince brought down. Couldn't take her eyes off it, she couldn't.

'Or off him,' added Henry. 'Quite put Mr Mulgrove's nose out of joint, it has. Oh, she's sweet on him all right. Our Miss Florence is sweet on a savage!'

A stunned silence had fallen over the servants' hall where, generally, dark skins were regarded with suspicion and in any case could have no possible connection with the tender passions. Especially where the gentry were concerned. The boot boy, who was cleaning the knives in the scullery, was heard to snigger. Mrs Maggot sharply ordered him outside. Henry should have held his tongue. Now it would be all over the village. None of them would be able to hold up their heads if that sort of talk got about, she said, and the servants' hall agreed.

The Honourable Florence Emily Ada was just eighteen; a milky blonde, looking milkier than ever that night, in white tarlatan and camellias. Her fiancé was considered eminently suitable, although only a second son. The family was immensely rich, with vast estates in the north. Edward was pleasant looking and of a studious bent. Archaeology was his passion, if any one so temperate could be said to have passions. He was in the service of the East India Company, largely because he was interested in Asiatic languages. He had lately been named to an important administrative post in Oudh, and was pressing that his marriage to Florence should be advanced so that he might take her back with him early in the New Year, before the real heat began.

'Fancy, Rosie!' Florence had said, 'He wants to go by the overland route so that we can spend our honeymoon at Mr Shepheard's famous hotel in Cairo and he can show me the Pyramids and the Sphinx.'

'Fancy, miss,' Rosie had replied dutifully, but privately she thought Mr Mulgrove a dull stick, and his interest in monuments misplaced on a honeymoon. Until a few days ago Florence had been quite satisfied with this project, finding in her fiancé, if not the dashing hero of those novelettes she devoured and sometimes passed on to Rosie, at least a suitable husband who would take her away from maternal tyranny and country stagnation; and whose life would lead her to those exotic climes which were so much discussed just then.

But ever since this house party had been announced it had seemed to Rosie that a change had come over her young mistress. She had been more capricious than ever, fussing over her clothes, washing her complexion in cucumber lotions and sleeping in curl papers and gloves soaked in whitening mixtures. As if that were necessary – she never does a hand's turn, thought Rosie, but without any particular bitterness. She did not envy Florence her way of life. She thought her own considerably more lively, which it certainly was. Rosie had been puzzled by Miss Florence's moodiness and all the rituals of beauty, until she heard the gossip of the servants' hall. Now she saw that Miss Florence was indeed out to captivate the foreigner prince and that Mr Edward's nose was properly out of joint.

That night, as she brushed Florence's long ash-blonde hair, her young lady had grown quite confidential. It appeared that Mr Edward was becoming very difficult. He'd even written to the Dowager, telling her she had no business to invite the Hindu prince down to Bogwood. 'Not to stay, that is,' said Florence. 'He says it simply is not possible to have the natives in the house.' (Just as if they were dogs, thought Rosie.) 'But you know how Mama is – the Rao was at the Duchess of

Sutherland's ball last summer – didn't I tell you how wonderful his jewels were and how I danced with him?'

'No, miss, I'm sure you didn't,' replied Rosie, discovering to her surprise that Florence could be secretive.

'Oh, I must have . . . Anyhow, Mama believes she can convert him, she wants to get his support for the orphanage, too. She's bought a beautifully bound Bible she's going to give him while he's here . . . Mama thinks, and I do too, that some people have been horrid to him – just because he's got a dark skin . . . As a matter of fact Mr Edward doesn't give a fig about Mama inviting him down – about it being incorrect, I mean. It's just because he's jealous. You know, the Rao is so very handsome and then, he's what they call a "nine tiger man" – that means he's a great hunter, he's killed nine tigers! I don't think Mr Edward has ever even seen one all the years he's been in India. Of course he's jealous! Why, he even tried to persuade Mama not to accept that lovely silver swing . . . And last summer there was a horrid scene at the Stafford House party when he snatched me away from the Rao right in the middle of a waltz. It was too provoking!' Her limpid glance faltered, and meeting Rosie's eyes in the mirror, she turned aside, looking suddenly sly.

She hasn't told me the half, thought Rosie, wielding the ivory-backed hairbrushes soothingly and content to wait. It would all come out, sooner or later. I must be careful, thought Florence, struggling to hide her true feelings while reliving, for the hundredth time, that wonderful evening at the Duchess of Sutherland's ball, where she felt her whole life had taken on a new meaning. Stafford House had been a worthy setting for this revelation. Floating up the great curved marble stairway towards her fate, buoyed up by an enormous crinoline, she had been dazzled by the chandeliers, the gilding and the magnificence of the scene. 'I come to your palace from my house,' Queen Victoria had said, driving over from Buckingham Palace to visit her friend the Duchess.

It happened as Florence was dancing a cotillion. She should have advanced, curtseyed, and chasséed sideways to where Edward was holding out a kid-gloved hand. But over his shoulder she had seen, in a blinding flash that was both light and darkness, a strange figure standing in the doorway, surrounded by a group of gentlemen. This disturbing creature shimmered from head to foot in cloth of gold, and his orange-coloured turban was tufted with a plume of fiery rubies that made the Duchess's tiara look like so many glass beads. But the brilliance of his costume and jewels seemed to Florence to pale beside the dark blaze of his eyes, and the quite overpowering effect of strength – of animal force – by which he appeared to dominate the scene.

Suddenly, and for the first time in her life, Florence was aware that beneath their clothes, men had bodies. Before the evening was over, she, like a number of other debutantes, had partnered the Rajput chieftain round the ballroom. But while all of them appeared quite mesmerized by their darkling cavalier, fluttering moth-like under his gaze and the watchful scrutiny of their men folk, Florence Emily Ada had almost fainted at the touch of his ungloved narrow brown hand, so narrow-boned for such a powerfully built man. Round each wrist Florence saw that he wore heavy jewelled bracelets, the stones set in a coloured enamel-work of flowers, but these did not make him appear effeminate, any more than the pear-shaped emeralds that hung from his ears, or the long blue-black locks which snaked on to his shoulders. He seemed an extraordinary mixture of contradictions, his eyes at once bold and sleepy, questing and indifferent. During the first turn around the ballroom Florence had wished passionately to sit out a dance with him – just one – in some secluded corner. Until now this had seemed the sum total of coquetry, but suddenly all was changed. She was in the grip of a great love. Her head spun, her mouth felt dry. She would die if she did not see him every day for ever after. This was real love! It was paradise, it was torment, it was unbearable, it was bliss . . .

At that precise moment Edward had appeared and made a scene; at least, a half-scene – just like Edward, nothing dramatic. . . He merely bowed, icily polite, and said, 'Forgive me, Prince, if I claim my fiancée for our last dance. Alas! We have to leave in a few moments.'

No explanations, no apologies. Florence had been too taken aback to oppose him. And anyway, how could she? He was her fiancé. And there was her mother, smiling amiably at the Rao as if nothing had happened. She was even beckoning him to her side. The Rao had bowed and relinquished Florence in a regrettably unconcerned way. Dancing woodenly round with Edward, she saw him bending over the Dowager in a most friendly manner. Could it be that Mama already knew him?

The Dowager had, in fact, met him a few weeks earlier in a box at the Opera. (*Rigoletto* – not quite suitable for young girls, said the mamas who ruled the London season, so Florence had not been present.) But the Dowager had found him most charming, *most* interested in her Missionary Society, and particularly encouraging about Edward's new post at Oudh, which it appeared he knew well. 'Not my born place, but I am hunting tiger there,' he had said in his endearing broken English. They had met again, once more at the Opera; *Traviata* this time – another of those subjects unsuitable for Florence whose musical education was thus becoming sadly neglected. But the Dowager had now taken one of her fancies to this handsome heathen – a brand to be snatched from the burning. Soon he was confiding his hopes and projects to her. There were many wrongs to be righted and grave injustices to be recognized. The Dowager decided to fight his battles for him in London, as, she fondly believed, he would (once converted) fight Christianity's battles on India's coral strand. Thus she had planned a house party where, as guest of honour, the Rao Jagnabad would have the opportunity to meet at leisure those highly-placed personages most likely to be useful to him in fighting for his rights.

The opposition of her future son-in-law was brushed aside. 'Not invite him down to Bogwood? My dear Edward, you may expect to guide and counsel Florence, your wife-to-be, but do not presume to give me advice. My mind is quite made up,' she said. Edward had to content himself by muttering that it would all end badly. He had remarked, as she had not, the startling effect which this Hindu had upon Florence.

No one knew or cared what effect the Hindu was having on Rosie as she stood there in the thin rain that was now falling, soaking through the shawl she clutched round her, and misting the park where the cows stood disconsolate under the dripping beeches. Rosie knew, with as much certainty and far more experience than Florence, that this was a man she wanted – must have – and moreover would have. However improbable, she knew that one day she and this stranger would come together. If she had known anything about the beliefs of the East she would have said: it is written.

Now she could see the guests on their feet, raising their glasses towards the Rajput chieftain. She saw again that proud, restive movement of the head, while the long, heavy-lidded eyes seemed to fix on something beyond the table, beyond the windows, as if, piercing the curtains, the window panes and the mists in which she stood, they reached some remote horizon which they alone could see. Rosie longed for them to focus upon herself, for him to become aware of the violence of her feelings.

Pressed against the glass she took a final, greedy look; it might have to last her a long while. The stranger was bending towards the Dowager; his dark face intent, harsh. Suddenly Rosie felt very cold. A nice cup of something hot, something with rum in it – that's what, she thought. She'd catch her death, standing there. Better go in now and get on with the work. And she'd make short work of William if he started any of his tricks in the pantry.

Later that night, getting her young lady undressed had been quite a business. She'd stood there as if turned to stone, having to be pulled and pushed and not uttering a word about the dinner party, until all of a sudden she'd jerked her head away from the hairbrush and turned on Rosie wildly.

'You've got to help me! D'you hear? I've got to see him alone. Who? Why, the Rao to be sure. Don't stand there gaping. Oh, Rosie, you don't know how I love him. I love him! I tell you, I love him! You've got to get this letter to him – now – tonight! I can't trust anyone but you.' Her voice rose shrilly and her hands trembled as she thrust a sealed envelope at Rosie.

'But, Miss Florence, it's long past midnight – how can I?' Rosie was quite thunderstruck by such an unladylike display of passion.

'You can! You must!' replied Florence, grown reckless with the heat of love. 'The gentlemen are still in the smoking room. They won't move for quite a while yet. You can creep along the corridor and slip it under his door. Mama has dismissed Polethorpe – no one is about.'

She leaned back, very pale, her hand pressed to her heart, in a gesture at once theatrical and instinctive. Indeed, she could feel it pounding beneath her fingers. Surely he would respond. He must! During the evening she had noticed him staring at her with a mysterious intensity. It was the unblinking stare of the hunter, or even the myopic, rather than the lover, but Florence was far too inexperienced to realize this. She had now decided that he did not dare avow his true feelings for her – after all, he was a native, even though a prince, while she was a young English lady and moreover, betrothed to another. But now all that would be changed. Tomorrow, knowing how she felt, he would be free to speak, to declare his love and to confront both Edward and Mama with the truth. There would be no denying such a love . . . She would sail for India, yes, but in his arms, as his wife . . . as the Rani! Such unimaginable vistas of bliss almost made her faint. She groped for her smelling salts.

'Are you quite all right, miss?' asked Rosie, whose own heart was thudding at the thought of what the unforeseen chances of this night might bring. She was of the nature to seize on, and profit by, the winds of chance. Now they were blowing her way.

Settling Florence in the chintz-hung bed and leaving the nightlight burning companionably, she stole from the room, Florence's letter concealed in her bodice. The corridor was quiet, but she could hear the gentlemen still laughing below. Looking down over the balustrade, she saw the bald top of Mr Brill's head as he prepared a line of silver candlesticks which he was hoping he would soon be able to hand each gentleman as he bowed him up to bed. It had been a long day for Brill, and when he heard them embark on the subject of the late Crimean campaigns he feared they would be there for another hour at least. He leaned against a plinth supporting a bust of the fifth Viscount, in Roman laurels, and took the weight off his feet.

Up on the first floor Rosie could hear the guests' various voices. Recalling the faces she had observed so closely through the conservatory windows, she now tried to fit each voice to its rightful face. Those of Mr George and Mr Edward were familiar, and there was little doubt that the pompous tones telling of victories were those of the Cabinet Minister, while the voice shouting about cavalry charges was unquestionably that of the Duke. She wondered what sort of voice the Hindu had, and if she would know it when she heard it. He'll talk foreign as likely as not, she thought, having no clear idea what this implied, for she had never encountered any foreigners as yet. She did not have long to wait, for the talk turned on the usual bugbear of that moment – alleged Russian aggression in the East and threats to the North West Frontier.

'Mark my words,' said a voice, 'those Russkis will give us trouble again. They've always had their eye on India.'

'Perhaps we should ask the Rao Jagnabad's opinion on that point.' Rosie recognized the speaker as Mr Edward. His voice sounded scornful, she thought, spiteful even. It was clear he was jealous of the handsome foreign visitor.

There was a moment's silence and then the Rao spoke, in a voice softer than Rosie had imagined, knowing only his harsh face. He spoke carefully, in that imperfect English which had such an irresistible appeal to so many of the ladies.

'Sahibs,' he said, 'you speak of battles and of Russia. My sorrow is to tell you your greatest battle shall be fought against your own armies – the Sipâhies – "Sepoys" you call them – my people, and that day is to come soon.' For a long moment no one spoke. Then the evening broke up in haste and formal cordialities.

The gentlemen filed out of the smoking room. Rosie drew back sharply from the balustrade and in a whisk of pink calico had slipped into the Rao's room. As the footsteps approached, she had suddenly known what she meant to do. She would give him the letter herself! Diving behind the bed curtains she stood hidden, breathless at her own audacity. She heard Mr George wishing his guest a very good night. Again that strangely spiteful note, a sort of careless patronage, too – the same way they spoke to her, or any of the other servants. 'Think you've got all you want for the night, Prince? I'll wager our houses seem pretty snug after those Indian bungalows, what?' The sound of a slap on the back. Silence from the stranger. Then the door opened and he entered the room. He turned the key behind him. Rosie sensed rather than heard him advance to the fireplace, where the large tin hip bath, then a customary object in well-ordered houses, was placed before the bright-burning logs; towels, sponges and soap spread round ritualistically.

There was no sound in the room and Rosie parted the curtains an inch to peer through. The Rao was standing before the hip bath, staring at it with an expression of profound distaste. The habits and hygiene of his own land were otherwise. Far more rigid rituals prevailed: there, bathing was regarded as either a religious rite, or a voluptuous delight of a social nature in vast marble tanks, or perfumed waterways cooled by lace-like marble lattices; but never, never in such a strange, severe and cramped receptacle, in such joyless circumstances.

He stood there morosely, kicking his embroidered yellow shoe against the unyielding brown-painted tin sides of the hip bath. Rosie was able to observe him closely. He was taller, broader, than she had thought and now, as he unwound the fifteen yards of elaborate gauze turban, she saw his black hair – black with a bluish sheen, like a raven's wing, she thought – fall on to his shoulders and merge with the short-curled beard that framed his face. Rosie liked beards: they were proper manly. She heard the clank of the heavy jewelled bracelets he wore and saw how sinewy his wrists were beneath them. Yes, a proper man all right, she thought, lost in admiration.

The stranger's skin was a dark, greenish-brown colour. As he unbuttoned his brocaded coat, Rosie saw he wore no shirt or under-vest – and that his body was as dark and gleaming as those statues of heathen gods Mr George had brought back from his travels. Rosie had the acute awareness of beauty so often to be found in persons of an amoral nature in whom the denials of the Church have not taken root. She followed the stranger's movements avidly as he unhooked the diamonds from his ears – worn, she noticed, not on the lobes, but on the ear tops – then unfastened the great pearl necklace, splashed rosewater over his face and hands, and began to unbuckle the jewelled belt of his baggy satin trousers. He had drawn them down over his narrow-boned bare feet and was sitting on the side of the bed in a muslin loincloth when Rosie sidled out from her hiding place, quite unabashed.

The Rao sprang up, his hand reaching for a small dagger which she saw was concealed in the folds of the loincloth. For a long moment they remained silent, appraising each other, the

Rajput chieftain in his loincloth and the English housemaid in her starched calico fortress.

'Goodness, sir, I don't mean to harm! Put that carving knife away, do, it fairly gives me the shivers,' said Rosie, as if it were the most natural thing in the world for her to be there, in his room, in the middle of the night.

Perhaps the stranger thought it was; thought it another, welcome aspect of English hospitality, for he smiled with a sudden unexpected sweetness, his heavy chiselled lips revealing magnificent teeth. He flung the dagger rattling on to the carpet and seized Rosie, unresisting, in his arms. When, a few minutes later, he was unbuttoning her bodice, Florence's letter crackled beneath his fingers and – like the dagger – was flung aside. Rosie made a half-hearted gesture towards it and even began to tell him it was the reason why she had come to his room. But he was not listening, and soon stopped her blabbing with his kisses.

Some hours later Rosie sat queen-like, enthroned and adorned, among the pillows and framed by the blue brocaded bed curtains. The firelight glowed on her flesh and the great pearls which cascaded over her bosom. Round her waist the Rao had fastened a chain of rubies, the biggest, pear-shaped drop hiding her navel, while her ankles were circled by his jewelled bracelets and her plump thighs wound with pearl-tasselled gold chains.

Rosie preened as the Rao held the mirror for her to see herself. (And to think she'd envied Miss Florence's seed pearls!) She studied herself again. She looked a treat. 'You are Rani,' said the Rao Jagnabad; placing his hands together in a ritual gesture of submission.

The first sour light of an autumn morning was seeping through the drawn curtains when Rosie opened her eyes and saw Florence's letter lying crumpled beside the dagger on the hearthrug. Drat! I ought to give it to him, she thought, and turned over to see the Rao lying very still beside her. But he was not asleep. The eyes of the bronze statue were wide open, watching her. She sat up, yawning and shivering. The room was bitter cold. Soon Lucy, the under housemaid, would be knocking on the door, expecting to come in and relight the fire. Rosie giggled at the thought of Lucy's face if she could have seen her wearing all that finery and nothing else . . . She must be off. Sliding out of the warm bed and kicking the letter towards the ashes, she dived into her chemise. But the bronze statue came suddenly to life. Frowning and imperious, he pulled it off again and dragged her down beside him.

'No clothes!' he commanded, and jerked the curtains closer round the bed. Once again Florence's letter lay unheeded.

II

'My word! Nearly nine, whatever have you been up to?' asked cook, who would have been very much surprised if Rosie had told her. But there was breakfast to be served – the gargantuan breakfast of those times – devilled kidneys, mutton chops, bacon and eggs, cold game pie, sausages, porridge and muffins, (preceded by morning prayers), so that once again, Rosie's absence was overlooked. She scuttled upstairs to wake Florence with a cup of tea, wondering what on earth she was going to tell her about the letter.

From the disorder in Florence's room it was clear that she too had passed a wakeful night. Her peignoir trailed on the ground beside a hairbrush and the latest novel, which had to be procured surreptitiously, for the Dowager strongly disapproved of such reading. The cover of the canaries' cage had slipped sideways, and they sat fluffed out in dudgeon. The writing table was in as much disorder as the dressing table, *pomades* among the envelopes, and pens among the hairpins. Florence turned her head aside resentfully as Rosie snapped up the blinds and the light fell on her red-rimmed eyes. Crying already, thought Rosie. I wonder how she'd carry on if she knew the truth. Florence sat up in bed, pushing aside the tea tray pettishly.

'My letter! What happened – did you get it to him?' The words spilled out uncontrollably, but as if ashamed; she did not meet Rosie's eye.

'To be sure I did,' replied Rosie, gaining confidence as she spoke. 'I left it right in the middle of his room. He's bound to have found it by now. Don't fret, Miss Florence, everything will come right, you'll see. I expect he'll be waiting for you downstairs . . . Perhaps he'll ask you to go for a walk with him, after luncheon.'

'Oh, do you really think so?' breathed Florence, reviving visibly at the prospect of wearing her new maroon tippet bordered with swansdown, as she and he, he and she – O the rapture! – made their escape from the rest of the guests – from Edward in particular, and were at last alone together in the conservatory, beside the swing – his lovely silver swing, with its carved tigers' heads and its seat like a little silver armchair all fringed in silver tassels . . . She imagined them there, together in the ferny jungle of the hot house – *his* climate, the heavy, scented tropics and *his* plants; the orchids and the trailing passion flower vines . . . She saw herself, her crinoline billowing up, allowing perhaps a glimpse of her booted ankle as, clinging to the silver ropes she was pushed higher and higher, to and fro . . . To his arms – and from them – and to them again, backwards and forwards, the dark, romantic and somehow deliciously frightening face of the Nine Tiger Man now near, now far, until he lifted her down and they sealed their love with their first kiss . . . O! The rapture! Mama – Edward – no one could stand in their way now. She sprang out of bed pink with excitement and was soon being laced into her corsets. Rosie, recalling the way the Rao Jagnabad had slashed her own stay-laces apart with his dagger, gave an extra tug, so that Florence winced.

'You'll want to look your best, won't you, miss?' she said, recalling her own reflection when the Rao had held the mirror for her to see her bare body hung with his jewels.

All that day Florence waited in an agony of indecision for the Rao Jagnabad to make some sign. But he made none. There had been church in the morning, which naturally he had not attended as the Dowager's conversion was still only a cherished project. Meanwhile, one of the house party had been detailed to keep him company.

Florence heard her brother and the gentlemen chaffing one another on the subject, 'Who'll volunteer to take the heathen for a walk this morning?'

'Don't show him the kennels, though, he thinks dogs are unclean.'

'What, skip church? I'm game, but how about the Dowager?'

'Oh, she'll be praying for both of you.'

Florence sat beside her mother in the family pew, simmering with impatience through the sermon ('Ask and it shall be given ye') and avoided Edward's tentative efforts to hold her hand on the walk back to Bogwood through the dripping muddy lanes. At luncheon (turbot, roast beef and rhubarb tart), the Rao had never once looked in her direction. Indeed, he had been taken up by a very dull discussion on land tenures in India and something about concessions due to him from the East India Company. The matter was quite beyond Florence's grasp, but of course *he* was right. She hated the way that stuffy Under Secretary smiled and the other gentlemen kept cutting in every time the Prince tried to explain. They seemed almost to be baiting him. They were horrid. Even Mama was unable to defend him now. They talked among themselves in that sarcastic way, as if he did not exist. She thought the Prince's dark eyes looked positively tragic as he studied each face, (except her own), intently, looking puzzled and sometimes having to ask someone to repeat something, for they drawled dreadfully, and Florence saw just how hard it was for him to follow all that was said. She could have plunged her knife into their starched shirt fronts there and then. Now they've driven him out for the rest of the day and I shall never get another chance to be alone with him – never, she thought bitterly, watching him galloping out from the stables, leaping the wall of the rose garden in a most reckless manner. She watched him out of sight, across the home park, her burning face pressed against the drawing room window down which the rain drops chased each other remorselessly. She was unaware, or uncaring, that Edward was eyeing her closely. When he drew her over to the piano and proposed that they should try out some new duets she could have boxed his ears.

'O, that we two were maying' they sang, soprano and baritone blending sweetly, and presently she allowed him to kiss her – one of Edward's diffident, boyish embraces, but she scarcely noticed, for her whole being was centred round a rider in a yellow turban, now setting the roan at a five-barred gate and laughing like a triumphant centaur as he galloped on.

So the day dragged by. That evening there was another dinner and more speeches and half promises by the Under Secretary for Foreign Affairs, who was cornered, but anxious to placate the Dowager, (such a close friend of the P.M.), to mislead the Rao, (altogether too sure of himself, must be kept from becoming too pressing), and to make positively no commitments that might conflict with the Honourable East India Company's interests, for he was one of the directors – a significant fact which he had not disclosed. Florence watched, in growing humiliation, for some sign of recognition from the Rao, but there was none – not a glance – and at bedtime she was thankful to snatch her candlestick and follow the rest of the ladies upstairs.

'You look tired out, dear child,' said her mother, absently patting her drooping shoulders. 'Perhaps, after all, I must give way to Edward and let you be married before he goes back to India . . . I don't like to see you fretting . . . We must think about your trousseau as soon as our guests have gone. Now let me see a smile. You've had that long face all day.' She rustled off, calling Polethorpe to unlace her.

Florence rushed into her room where Rosie was waiting, and without more ado burst into tears of mortification and despair.

Rosie counselled patience.

'Those foreign gentlemen, we don't know what's going on in

their heads, do we, miss?' she coaxed. 'Now, perhaps this very minute he's writing to you. Or perhaps he's waiting till it's all quiet and he'll come here tonight! Yes, here, like in the play about Romeo and Julia . . . perhaps he'll climb in at the window . . . I shouldn't be surprised at anything with those foreigners,' she added, quite astonished at her own duplicity, for she knew that the Hindu would be otherwise occupied. He had made her promise to return to him at midnight and she had every intention of gratifying both their wishes.

'Perhaps you should write him another letter,' she suggested. 'Perhaps, after all, he missed the first. I could try to be certain he got this one,' she volunteered. But Florence shook her head. She had already dared all, humbled herself and broken every canon of modesty and breeding. Something had gone wrong. What, she could not tell. There was nothing for it now but to plead a sick headache in the morning, thus avoiding the embarrassment of leave takings . . . And then to marry Edward just as soon as possible, and forget the whole humiliating business. An even more humiliating thought struck her. Was it possible that somehow she hoped their paths might cross again in India? Was she, Florence Emily Ada, really so wicked as to wish to marry one man in order to reach another? She put this shocking thought from her.

In the darkness and lying beside the Rao, Rosie knew that no man was ever again going to matter to her as did this unknown, come-by-chance lover. She grimaced, remembering all those clumsy caresses which had seemed a rather jolly part of life until now. William's fumblings, Mr Brill's pinches and the squalid importuning of the village boys . . . Enclosed in a blue-curtained world apart, Rosie knew, with a sinking heart, that Fate had set a term to her joys. Tomorrow the Hindu prince would leave, would vanish from her life, and there was no way, no way at all, to stay in his arms.

And so it was. Monday morning dawned, overcast and blustering. As the household assembled in the dining room for prayers, a lamp had to be placed beside the great family Bible from which the Dowager was reading the collect for the day before leading them in a hymn.

'Jesus, Saviour, pilot me
Over life's tempestuous sea.'

She sang robustly, yet the other voices sounded wan on the morning air. The servants joined in sullenly, but they knew better than not to appear devout. The Dowager would tolerate no half-hearted Christians in her household. The fire had not long been lit, and smoked, so that the singers coughed. Brill noted that the coals were badly laid and he smacked his lips in anticipation of the punishment he was going to dole out to Lucy when he got that young person alone.

Beyond the looped Brussels lace curtains, the sodden green lawns were speckled with birds tugging at worms. Guests and staff alike knelt in attitudes of devotion for the last prayer, but all of them were peeping through their fingers, eyeing each other, or the rain. For one, it spelled good hunting; for another rheumatism. William thought it would be too wet to spend long in the haystack with Rosie that night. Rosie noticed that Miss Florence's place was empty. So she hadn't the guts to come down to corner the Prince, thought Rosie, who had guessed correctly that the fatal letter had not been read or even seen by the Rao; it had, in fact, been used by Lucy to light the fire. From where she knelt, Rosie could see into the hall, where the Rao was being instructed how to tap and read the barometer by a fellow guest who, being a Roman Catholic, did not choose to kneel in worship beside Protestants. The Rao Jagnabad was looking puzzled. Since it rained continuously in England, it seemed scarcely worthwhile to consult this oracle, but he had observed that the English were most punctilious in their attentions.

Soon the carriages were at the door. One by one the guests

took their leave and were driven to the station. From the attic windows of the sewing room Rosie watched. And below, from behind the drawn curtains her headache imposed, Florence also watched. The Dowager knew how to convey to each guest her precise estimation of his worth by the choice of vehicle in which he was conveyed to or from the station. Her stables and equipages were kept up in almost as much style as during the lifetime of her husband, a celebrated figure of the Turf. Thus the Cabinet Minister went in the barouche; the Lord and Lady Mayoress in the britzka; the Admiral and the Judge in the brake.

The Italian Ambassador and his wife felt the status conferred by the landau was considerably diminished when the five-times-widowed beauty was packed in too. But the Ambassador revenged himself by refusing to sit back to the horses. 'It could be taken as a slight to my country, dear lady, you will understand . . . I must be first my country's representative and only then a man,' he said, sighing, and casting a lingering glance over the widow's corsage as she settled herself huffily, facing him. This had been a particularly telling piece of placement on the Dowager's part, for it reminded the Italian Ambassador of what she thought of Italy, while leaving the widow in no doubt as to her hostess's views, (which she shared with Queen Victoria), on the remarriage of widows.

The Under Secretary for Foreign Affairs, on a later train than the Cabinet Minister, shared with him the honours of the barouche, both returning to London in a glow of self esteem, for they had kept the Indian fellow in his place and made him realize he couldn't push the Government around; and he'd better not go on hoping any of those paltry claims would be recognized by Britain. Nevertheless, it was the family state coach, no less, which was reserved for the Rao Jagnabad. This was generally kept in London, in the stables of the town house, and only brought out for a Court ball or some splendid occasion. But now the Dowager had ordered it down to

Bogwood, expressly for the use of her sable protégé. As the cumbersome vehicle was driven through the narrow lanes, the villagers turned out to gape, as much at its canary-yellow carriage-work, emblazoned panels and fringed olive green hammer cloth, as at its occupant – this glittering, improbable figure glimpsed within.

From the first floor windows and the attic respectively, Florence and Rosie now saw the Rao emerge, careless of the rain, in crimson and gold brocade and then turn back to fall on one knee, clasping the Dowager's hand. With an unexpected, supple movement, he bent low and laid his head across her foot. It was a most touching Oriental gesture of love, submission and gratitude. This visit on which he had pinned his hopes had not turned out well. He had been snubbed by these English gentlemen in their own arrogant way. Oh, most civil, but they had known just how to infer that for them he was a savage and his claims absurd. It was not his hostess's fault. She had done her best for him. He felt a surge of true emotion as he pressed his lips to the instep of her kid boot. The Dowager was visibly moved. She too realized that none of her carefully chosen guests intended to support his claims, (she must cut the Cabinet Minister as soon as the occasion presented itself. As for the Under Secretary, she would see to it that he heard what people were saying about his wife and that vulgar banker from Hamburg), but there was really nothing more she could do for the Rao's cause here. She looked down at the turbaned head laid so affectionately low and was visibly moved.

'My dear boy, my dear son,' she murmured, raising him in motherly arms. She had every confidence that he would propagate the Gospel for her on his return to India.

No doubt it was now only a matter of time before he would be received into the Church. His donation to the orphanage had been more than lavish, and the curiously woven basket which served him as luggage, she knew contained the Bible she had given him. Gratified, she watched his carriage disappear round a turn in the drive. Ungratified, her daughter saw it go with anguish in her heart.

As for Rosie, determination grew within her. The stranger had come out of India and would go back. She must contrive to get there, to find him again; to find the wild, terrible and beautiful face of love he had revealed.

III

Florence's marriage to Edward Mulgrove was celebrated in London with due circumstance. At the beginning of 1857 they left for India. Rosie accompanied them as Florence's personal maid. Neither the Dowager, nor Polethorpe, had thought her sufficiently experienced, but Florence had shown unusual obstinacy in this matter. Rosie had known just how to insist. It would never do if the business of the letter came out, she said, and Florence had hurriedly agreed.

The overland voyage across France went smoothly. Every morning Rosie wakened her master and mistress with a brew of tea which she personally prepared in the various hotel kitchens. Usually she surprised Mr Edward asleep, but Miss Florence, as she still called her, was mostly awake, looking limp and fidgety and complaining of headaches. Rosie, who sometimes encouraged the French *valets de chambre*, or fellow travellers, had no patience with such vapourings. However, it would not do to get on the wrong side of her mistress – not yet. Not until they reached India, anyhow.

The journey was taking quite a time. Edward had insisted on staying more than a week at both Avignon and Nimes, spending whole days dragging Florence, and sometimes Rosie, up and down Papal stairways and across Roman arenas. Perhaps, finding Florence an unresponsive bride, he was even then unconsciously compensating himself by archaeological excesses. The two women listened to long-winded breakfast lectures on what they were to see that day, so that Florence's migraine came on regularly, before they had even started out. Rosie toiled behind the Mulgroves, carrying green-lined parasols, the picnic basket, and other tourist impedimenta, but looking about her with lively curiosity, her eyes narrowed in the strong sunlight. She thought she was going to enjoy the East even more.

On reaching Cairo, Florence was prostrated by the extreme heat, the dust and noise. She found the Pyramids far too steep and was dragged up like a protesting sack. The tombs of the Mamelukes, like the Sphinx, meant little to her. Neither did they to Rosie, but it was a nice outing all the same and some of the Egyptians were likely-looking lads in their scarlet tarboosh, their brown necks rising from their white draperies like bronze columns and reminding her of the Rao, so she smiled at them, her wide childish smile, and took it as fun when they fumbled impudently with her skirts as they settled her a top a camel.

Edward would have liked to linger in Cairo, for some particularly interesting excavations were about to begin, but Florence was entirely unnerved by a quite unforeseen occurrence. Three young wives of Indian Army officers had arrived at the hotel within days of each other – all of them in an interesting condition and on their way back to England, anxious to avoid being confined in the conditions prevailing in the Deccan, the Punjab, or wherever their husbands were stationed. Now, by some singular chance, within a week, as if encouraged by the comforts of Shepheard's Hotel, all three of them were taken short and brought to bed there. Only a year before they had been brides, on their way out, like Florence. Now their shrieks and groans were rending the air. It was terrible! It gave poor Mrs Shepheard a lot of extra work and exasperated her husband, for it quite cast a blight over the hotel guests, until the sufferers were pronounced on the mend and the squalling babies paraded in triumph. But Florence had identified herself with every pang and could not be calmed. So this was to be her lot! Why had she ever married Edward and left England? 'Oh Mama!' she sobbed, and Edward felt a brute.

'Now, Miss Florence – madam, I mean – don't take on so,' said Rosie comfortingly. 'Some ladies have a very easy time, like shelling peas out a pod it is with some. It doesn't follow you'll have to go through all this . . . Why, you may never even have one,' she added. But Florence only sobbed louder, for she had been brought up to think child-bearing was a wife's first duty, and a childless woman cursed. This was the only concept she shared with the East she was now approaching.

Cairo, Alexandria – and at last Bombay, with its tall palms fringing the beaches, where the graceful, strangely rigged Arab dhows sailed in, spice-laden, from Zanzibar across the Arabian Ocean. Once on Indian soil, Edward assumed a new stature and it was seen he was of considerable consequence, being treated with the greatest respect by both the British and the natives. And it was truly impressive to see with what ease he switched from one dialect or language to another – Hindu, Tamil, Pushtu, Marathi and even Persian. They travelled up country, through dark green groves of mangoes, across expanses of sand; hill country of the utmost savage desolation, or jungles where even Edward at his most reassuring could not deny that tigers lurked. Florence and Rosie travelled in palkis – box litters carried jerkily by bearers – but Edward rode and sometimes went on ahead looking for game. Florence remembered that the Rao Jagnabad – whom she endeavoured to banish from her thoughts – was a 'nine tiger man,' and she prayed that Edward was able to defend them.

Now, in the midst of this alarming landscape, she remembered other things she would rather have forgotten. She remembered a day when she and George had accompanied Edward to the East India House Museum in Leadenhall Street. While Edward had been looking something up in the Library, George had offered to show her Tippoo's Tiger. 'Quite a curiosity,' said George. He explained how it had been captured by the British at Seringapatam in 1799, when Tipu Sultan, the ruler of Mysore, 'a most blood thirsty ruffian,' was defeated and killed. But not before he'd slaughtered and tortured hundreds of innocent Europeans, it was said. He had a fearful hatred of the English, objecting – perhaps not unnaturally – to their encroachment on Indian soil. As much as he abhorred the English, he revered tigers, surrounding them with a mystical aura and even identifying himself with these ferocious beasts. He saw them as the saviours of his country, avenging tawny angels, and his palace walls were frescoed with caricatures of trembling English being torn to pieces by obliging tigers. But his greatest delight was a mechanical organ with clockwork figures, almost life-size, representing a Bengal tiger savaging a prostrate white missionary.

This ghoulish piece of mechanism could be wound up, at which a musical box concealed inside the tiger uttered a series of deafening roars, while the missionary shrieked. These sounds were accompanied by a series of convulsive movements made by the victim's arm jerking up and down in a most realistic manner, as if imploring the mercy of heaven, if not of the tiger. George had wound up the 'Man-Tiger-Organ', but Florence had fainted outright at the first shrieks and growls.

Now they rang in her ears every time Edward left her side. When he went off shooting, she always lay in the stifling litter with her eyes tight shut till he returned. She would fasten the curtains round, as if their bleached cotton folds could secure her from the horrors outside. But Rosie looked about her, trying to talk with the bearers and beginning to pick up a few words of the local dialects as she sampled the foods they prepared at night over the camp fires, which were lit as much to keep away the wild beasts as to heat anything.

They went slowly northwards through villages where clay-daubed fakirs sat under the shivering peepul trees, staring angrily at nothing, and packs of mangy dogs and skinny children started up from the dust to clamour round them. Rosie always begged to be allowed to get out, to climb the steps of the gold-roofed, banner-hung temples, to smell the moghra flowers, and to feed the chattering swarms of monkeys hurtling through the trees. This was India – the Rao Jagnabad's country – and each time they passed under the great stone gates of another town she wondered if she would suddenly see him before her in all his pride, riding on a bedizened elephant shaded by a pearl-fringed umbrella, as she had seen in Miss Florence's picture books of India, over which she had poured ever since that October night, (so long ago it seemed now), when she had first set eyes on the Rajput prince.

'Rosie has quite taken to India,' Edward told Florence who merely pursed her lips. The movement of the palki made her queasy and she had long ago decided that her feelings for the Rao Jagnabad were not strong enough to overcome the discomforts and terrors she was enduring on this interminable journey.

At last Delhi was reached, and with it, the ameliorations of life among the British, who feted Florence as the newest bride. Beneath the towering crimson walls of the Red Fort, the English Club clung; incongruously modest – offering cards, conversation, iced claret and, occasionally, a ball. The Mulgroves were installed in a house outside the city, beyond the Kashmir Gate. It belonged to old friends of Edward's, now absent up country. It was a spacious white-pillared bungalow surrounded by burnt-up lawns, but shaded by fine trees. All night the little stripe-backed chipmunks disputed shrilly, and the watchmen patrolled the wide verandahs striking the ground with their iron-tipped staves, sounding a peculiar double rap said to keep the cobras away. Even so, these terrifying creatures were forever in evidence, either being caught and killed by the servants, or emerging swaying and baleful from baskets brought by their charmers, who seemed to think Florence must wish to watch them.

Combats between snake and mongoose were constantly proposed. Florence became thoroughly unpopular when she paid to have this spectacle removed from her sight. The servants would glare, done out of their treat by their spoilsport memsahib; and the snake charmers would *salaam* sullenly, arresting their nerve-racking, two-note music as on a strangled cry, shuffling off with their heaving sacks of vipers or mongooses slung across their shoulders. They scowled now when they passed the bungalow. They had been paid, yes, but their art had been rejected.

Beyond the orange groves and sinjib trees surrounding the house, Florence could see the spine of a sprawling red rock hill known as the Ridge. It shimmered in the sunlight, its rose quartz surface giving off a feverish glare. It was topped by two landmarks – Flagstaff Tower, where the Union Jack stirred languidly in the hot wind; and further south, a handsome house in the Mogul Gothic style, known as Hindu Rao's house.

Hindu *Rao*? Florence's heart jumped painfully every time it was mentioned. For one suffocating moment she had thought it might be *his* house. Since she had been settled in Delhi and the fatigues of the journey were behind her, both her health and her romantic memories had revived. She found that she still thought, with a mixture of shame and longing, of the Rao Jagnabad. She made some elaborately careless enquiries, (when Edward was not there of course), but none of the English seemed to have heard of him. Native princes are two a penny, they told her. Hindu Rao had been some Maratha chieftain, they said. Now his house was inhabited by an English official. Once, said Edward, it had been the site of Timour's tent when, with his Tartar hordes, he laid siege to Delhi. But even this did not rouse Florence. She was neither historically nor archaeologically minded. In vain Edward took her to the tombs of Safdah Jung and the Emperor Humayon, or to the Qutab Minar to view the city from its topmost balconies. It merely gave Florence vertigo. In vain he took her shopping, searching out Mogul miniatures; Florence thought some of the subjects very odd; and when he pointed out how the graceful swelling domes of the Pearl Mosque were echoed in the curved flank of a jade sherbet ewer, or, he suggested – greatly daring – by a woman's breasts, Florence coloured, but remained apathetic. Edward could only hope she would take more kindly to life at Oudh.

Soon they must be going there. Dutifully, Florence began to study Murray's *Hindu-English Phrase Book*. Most of it was in the imperative tense: 'Tell that person to get out of my way!' 'Bid these people give over their noise till I get past!' 'As you value your place, have the Sahib's trousers shortened in an hour!' Further down the page a more sombre note was struck. Florence read with misgiving: 'Does this horse stand gunfire?' 'Has any sick person slept in this bed lately?' 'Tell him I am attacked with cholera.'

The book dropped from Florence's limp hand and she lay under her mosquito netting, overcome with homesickness.

Not so Rosie. She had discovered life in Delhi offered undreamed-of possibilities for pleasure. She had picked up with an Irish sergeant in the 38th Native Infantry stationed out at the cantonments north of the Ridge. Soon he was enslaved, hanging around the Mulgroves' bungalow at all hours. Rosie made him take her driving in a tonga – a little cart with a fringed awning and tufts of coloured feathers decorating the shafts. They would go spanking down the Chandni Chowk, principal thoroughfare of the Mogul city, where dark alleys led to the silversmiths' bazaars and booths where they sold sweetmeats, spices and tinselled gewgaws; and where, in the street consecrated to marriage ornaments, the white horses stood caparisoned in crimson velvet and gold, waiting to carry the bridegrooms who would that night be conducted with pomp to their eager brides. It was a world of the senses – a world which Rosie understood.

At dusk women roused themselves from the torpor of the

day's heat and began to adorn themselves. Men sprawled in the doorways already lost in unshared worlds of delight, chewing betel nut, or smoking bhang, the bluish smoke from their hookahs drifting in wraiths, or mounting slowly to the fretted and painted houses overhanging the alleyways. From barred, cage-like balconies above, the raucous cries of the prostitutes sounded as they twitted the passing crowds. Some of them recognized the Irish sergeant as he strutted by, and they were calling him to join them. He was well known in this quarter – the Chakla Shäitanpura, or Devil's town, as it was called. He was a free spender who enjoyed dicing and quail-fighting with the men of the quarter – with those who were not too strict about an Infidel's shadow falling on them, that is. Hereabouts, free spenders like the sergeant often overcame such scruples. But now the Irishman was plainly uneasy beneath his swagger, for he had Rosie hanging on his arm. A white woman in the Randi Bazaar! She had persuaded him to take her deep into the old town, and now she was smiling and dawdling along as if she was at a fair, bold as brass, peering into the booths, jostling with the crowds. He didn't know another woman who'd dare. Holy Mary! If any of his officers were to see them there he'd be flogged, likely as not. 'Come away, me darlin' girl,' he pleaded, but Rosie only laughed and presently started wheedling him to take her upstairs, to one of the establishments where the jasmine-garlanded dancers plied their trade.

But this the sergeant had refused stoutly. The idea! She was an odd one and no error. Soon he found it more prudent to loose her to a corporal in the 9th Lancers, taking up himself with a nice quiet girl who was an apothecary's daughter by the Ajmeer Gate.

Rosie was not in the least put out. She knew what she wanted and soon her impudent charm had worked on a dandified young Eurasian, a well-to-do cloth merchant's son. He found her curiosity agreeably stimulating and at night he would wait for her under the big banyan tree by the gate. She would steal out enveloped in a burqa – the long white cotton cloak worn by the Muslim women, a tent-like affair designed to maintain the strict purdah of their lives. From behind the close-netted eyepiece Rosie's green eyes gleamed bright in the starlight as she climbed into the Eurasian's gig and they rattled off towards the Chandni Chowk, and in particular, towards the secrets of Shäitanpura, those secrets which so intrigued Rosie.

The Eurasian paid the old madams well when he took the woman in the burqa upstairs and he, in turn, was well satisfied with what she offered him in the small deep-cushioned alcoves behind the arched room where the nautch dancers undulated and postured to the sound of flute and drum.

Sometimes Rosie pushed him aside to join the women sipping tea, puffing at their rosewater hookahs and awaiting their admirers. Surprisingly, she was beginning to understand something of their speech and ways, and she would try out the hookahs and persuade them to show her how to wind a sari, paint her feet and hands vermilion, and to teach her the posturing tricks of their trade. All of India seemed to fascinate her – particularly its *vie galante*. The Eurasian could not make her out. He had always understood English women did not care for that sort of thing. Certainly the few ladies who condescended to dance with him at the Club were not encouraging. His mother, a beauty from Mysore, had caught his father, the cloth merchant, by such wiles. However, his father had always insisted that with white ladies it was different.

But then Rosie was no lady. Sometimes it seemed as if she didn't care if he were there or not. Could she be *using* him? It was unthinkable . . . And yet . . . He had given her one of those traditional mirrored rings, a round of looking glass set in a frame of gilt filigree which a bride wore on her thumb and by which she could catch over her shoulder, as if by chance, a first glimpse of her husband-to-be. He had explained the little bauble to Rosie when they had seen it in a jeweller's booth off the Chandni Chowk and nothing would do: he must buy it for her. Now she was forever toying with it, holding it up to those laughing green eyes, squinting into it, as if to catch sight of the Great Mogul, no less. How could he know that Rosie still hoped she would find the Rao Jagnabad? She still believed that one day, wandering through the bazaars, on the steps of the Musjid Jumma, or here, in the jasmine-scented twilight of Mother Baghmati's establishment, she would come on him again . . . That one day, as she gazed into the little thumb ring, he would appear behind her, as if summoned by a spell – by the spell of her longing.

Sometimes in her droll but comprehensible Hindi she questioned the girls about the Rao Jagnabad. But they only shook their sleek black heads. So many men came and went. Sikhs, Sepoys, Pathans, men from the north and south, Rajput warriors – perhaps he had been among them – Persian traders, money -lenders, cut throats, layabouts, princes of the blood – of the House of Timour even. So long as they paid, no one remembered them in the Chakla, where these houses of pleasure were located.

Presently Rosie found the presence of her Eurasian lover becoming irksome. There were finer men, fiercer, more handsome creatures to be met with in Shäitanpura: men who reminded her of the Rao Jagnabad. She knew her way there well enough by now, and she was well enough known to the madams, too. What did she care what they thought of her? Her money was as good as another's. She'd saved her wages for the last two years and now she'd spend them as she pleased. Rosie never stopped to count the cost of anything she'd set her mind on. Now she decided to shake off the Eurasian, but this was more difficult than she had supposed, for he was of a clinging nature. At last one of the girls at old Baghmati's establishment provided a draught largely composed of powdered glass, which kept him critically ill, with no heart for loving, for quite a while.

Now Rosie could roam, fancy free. The burqa told no tales and her nocturnal comings and goings went unremarked, or unreported, in the bungalow where the Mulgroves still lingered. Rosie had her own ways of silencing both the night watchman and the water carrier who slept by the gate. Untouchables were they? Rosie smiled to herself. She'd found them touchable all right she thought, and laughed aloud, her jolly, childish laugh. She was enjoying her own beauty and the powers it gave her over all men.

All through the gathering heat of April, Rosie lived this strange counterpoint. Her mornings were spent coddling Miss Florence – threading ribbons through her caps, dabbing her with *eau de Cologne*, or making baked custards or arrowroot, the better to thwart those disorders which the inescapable curries imposed on Florence. Afternoons were spent dozing, restless, beneath punkahs which fanned tepid air over them. At dinner time, in the cool of the evening, the British Colony met at one another's houses, or the Club, for dinner and whist. But they were not late evenings. By eleven o'clock Florence was generally settled for the night. Under the looped mosquito nets, Edward lay beside her reading aloud about the ancient wisdoms of India, although carefully avoiding references to the Kama Sutra or any of the erotic cults and symbols which play so large a part in Indian religion. Then Rosie would steal out, muffled in the burqa, to where, under the snake-like hanging roots of the banyan tree, one of Mother Baghmati's servants would be waiting in a tonga, ready to conduct her to Shäitanpura.

Nothing was too much trouble if it suited the woman in the burqa, said Baghmati to her girls. The Ferenghi – the foreigner – paid well for her pleasures and, said Baghmati, looking cunning, she pleased the men, too. There were plenty of gold pieces left in the bowl by the door since she'd been coming there. But it was just as well she – Baghmati – had thought up the notion that the Ferenghi shouldn't speak. Best pass her off as a mute – a Circassian slave girl who'd got out of Turkey, perhaps; with those green eyes she could easily be Turkish, too. Anything, so long as no one suspected she was British. That could lead to a lot of trouble just now, said the old procuress thoughtfully, chewing betel nut and fondling a parakeet which tumbled and crawled about her person.

So Rosie, silent and satiated, passed her nights in Shäitanpura, learning those arts of love by which the East has always set such store, and which she believed would one day conjure the Rao Jagnabad – and keep him forever in her arms.

It was the beginning of May, high time the Mulgroves left for Oudh, where Edward's new post awaited him. Both Florence and Rosie disliked the prospect. For Florence, it was another move, to drag her deeper, more irrevocably into this alien land of terror, heat and loneliness. For Rosie, it spelled the end of all those diversions which she had found in the alleyways of the Mogul city. The two women began checking the tin-lined trunks and household supplies they had brought out with them: barriers, which Florence and most of the British erected between themselves and India.

'One case marmalade, ditto Gentleman's Relish,' read Rosie. 'One crate light ale. Two dozen claret. Twenty-four linen sheets. Six damask tablecloths . . .' Glancing aside, she noticed the house boys were sluicing down the tattis, reed blinds which smelled sweet when wetted, but the boys were working in a slipshod manner. It was certainly very hot. Rosie told them to get the big punkah going. 'And bring lemonade for memsahib,' she ordered the ayah, seeing Florence's face. She herself did not feel the heat greatly. Her hair hung in damp ringlets, but otherwise she looked as pert and inviting as ever. She had quite taken over the household management, leaving Florence free to lie on the sofa gasping like a landed fish. Rosie had no sympathy with her these days.

She was helping Florence change her crumpled wrapper for a fresh one, which after an hour of such heat would be as crumpled, when Edward Mulgrove hurried into the room. He looked harassed. 'Better get all this baggage done quickly, my love,' he said, bending to kiss Florence's clammy brow. 'We shall have to leave almost at once. There is trouble. I didn't want to tell you before. The Sepoys have mutinied at Meerut. Shocking affair. They shot down their officers and turned on the civilians. They are said to be on their way here. News has just been telegraphed through. It looks serious.'

That was the tenth of May. On the eleventh, two thousand rebel cavalry clattered over the bridge of boats across Jumna river beside the Red Fort and streamed into Delhi unchecked. The British had only a token military force in the capital. Under their noses, the mutineers proclaimed the puppet King, the aged Bahadur Shah, their Emperor, and set about slaughtering all the British they could find. In the Guard House of the Red Fort Captain Douglas, the Guard Commander, was shot down. Commissioner Fraser and the Rev. Midgley Jennings who were visiting him were hacked to pieces, while the missionary's daughter was dragged from her hiding place in a wardrobe and battered to death. On the roof of the Delhi and London Bank, the manager held back the mob desperately, his wife beside him, armed only with a hog spear, but they were soon overwhelmed and perished horribly. The Mutiny was beginning as it was to continue – at Cawnpore, and Lucknow and Delhi and so many other places – in terror and bloodshed, and unimaginable cruelties on both sides.

IV

Edward showed a most unexpected dispatch and got them clear of Delhi that same night, making his way south towards Agra. All day those of the British who had not already been set on by the mob were fleeing out of the city northwards, stumbling lines of bewildered civilians seeking the protection of a handful of soldiers, almost as bewildered, on the Ridge. By noon it was known that the telegraph wires were cut between Delhi and Meerut, from where it was believed reinforcements must arrive at any moment. Yet no help came, for inexplicably, no orders had been given for the powerful Meerut garrison to pursue the rebels. Delhi stood alone. By the afternoon, a handful of British soldiers had blown up the magazine in a desperate bid to prevent supplies of ammunition falling into rebel hands. But in the heart of the Mogul city the Sepoys had their reserves. Now they were gathering along the walls facing the Ridge, and from that vantage point, or from the roofs and windows of the houses, they were picking off the straggle of British who were still trying to make their way to the Flagstaff Tower, crouching in the scrub wastes, dodging, breaking cover, doubling and dying like the hunted game they had become.

For those who had reached the British lines, or were as yet beyond the range of snipers' bullets, nothing was now left but indecision, terror, helplessness and blind courage. Some, like Edward Mulgrove, decided to risk all, in an attempt to escape across a country they did not yet know was ripe for rebellion. Some stayed, in arrogance, believing that to be British was to be unassailable. Some perished before they could assess their situation. Some survived, to be haunted for the rest of their lives by the memory of that time.

Edward, his wife, Rosie and two bearers – Sikhs who had

been with Edward since his first days in India and now remained loyal – set out at dusk. The women rode in a bullock palki, the box litter slung between two lumbering and despondent-looking animals. It was decided that the only hope of escape lay in passing boldly, with no air of haste or flight, and wearing native clothes. At a distance, in the depth of a curtained palki, even the memsahibs, in burqas, might pass unremarked, said the bearers, who were insistent. Edward shrugged. It was worth trying, he agreed, grimly buckling a revolver beneath the long padded atamsouk he wore in his role of Persian merchant. He planned to escort the women to Azampur, a small garrison town south of Agra which he believed to be outside the periphery of any significant military operations. Here he imagined he could leave them in comparative safety and make his own way across country to the kingdom of Oudh, to the post he had not yet joined. Or, if the rebellion was spreading, as he feared it might, he would head for Lucknow and place himself at the disposition of the British Resident.

The bearers, adjusting his turban with loving care, had rehearsed him in his role. 'You are Roullah Khan, a Persian merchant from Lahore, sahib, and the memsahibs are your wives. You are taking the dead body of your father-in-law to Agra to bury him beside his ancestors. Your pious journey will be respected.' Florence stifled a scream as she saw the unmistakably shaped bundle, a long roll of swathed cotton and matting, roped across the back of a camel standing in lofty detachment beside the litter.

My word, a real live corpse! thought Rosie, whose sense of humour was of a crude order. Her spirits were rising irrepressibly at the prospect of adventure. They were setting out to travel through this country which enthralled her, and with the optimism bred of a perfect digestion, she was already discounting the dangers.

It had been no trouble, no trouble at all, getting hold of a body, said the Sikhs in answer to Edward's questioning. The ditches outside the Ajmeer Gate were filling up with the dead and dying English. The mob, relishing their unexpected power, were still hacking at them as they lay there. Edward found himself wondering whose body they carried with them, that of a man or a woman? Of a friend, almost certainly, for the European colony was small and well known to one another. His horse plunged and reared in sudden fright as the camel broke into a lumbering trot, causing the long package to lurch sideways, almost unseating him.

Edward saw, with wry amusement, his wife's hands emerge briefly from the depths of the palki in an effort to secure the curtains closer. Those white ineffectual hands of hers which scarcely seemed able to press ferns in an album were now loaded with barbaric silver ornaments, tinted vermilion and clutching convulsively at the curtaining. The weeping ayah had produced her own ornaments, but her bungling panic had exasperated Rosie, who pushed her aside to stain both her own and Florence's hands and feet expertly. This being something she had learned from Baghmati's girls, it was fortunate that, in the tension of the moment, no one thought to enquire how she came by such skill. As wives of a Persian, both of them wore burqas over cotton trousers, the customary chalvar of the Muslim woman. Rosie had produced her own burqa, to which she now attached an almost superstitious importance. (It brings me good luck, she thought naïvely; and certainly it brought her good times.) Now, dragging it over her head, adjusting the round mask-like eyepieces, she felt at ease, as if in her own world, or sphere of adventure. Like a privateer in full sail charting new seas, she climbed confidently into the palki.

The little party followed the sandy expanses of the river bed and skirted the Palace walls unremarked. Incredibly, the road below Bahadur Shah's fretted marble pavilions stretched ahead, empty. No sentries challenged them from the turrets of the Red Fort, nor did they meet with any troops as they drew level with the great bulk of Humayon's Tomb, where they picked up the

Agra road. The few peasants or lone riders they passed were all heading towards the city and gave no thought to the Persians' slow-moving party. They were set on joining the mutineers within the walls, to taste with them the first fruits of victory and to fling themselves in waves of pent-up hatred on the houses of the Europeans, hounding down the trapped inhabitants in cruel play before they finished them off, one way or another, and settled down to the plunder. There was plenty of such sport to be had in the city and as yet there were no organized patrols out on the roads.

As each landmark passed safely – Humayon's Tomb, the Qutab Minar, the Lodi Tombs – Edward could not believe that their luck still held. Some years of studying the Hindu philosophers had inclined him to their fatalistic beliefs. Perhaps it was indeed written, and for some inscrutable design they were destined to survive while others died. Afterwards, long afterwards, Edward used to think it might have been better if they had all perished in Delhi. But these reflections still lay a long way ahead – beyond Azampur, beyond the distant line of hills enclosing that Rajput kingdom where Rosie and his wife were to act out the interwoven drama of their lives.

It was a densely black night, lit only by the fires of gipsy encampments which dotted the wastes among crumbling memorials to forgotten princes. These wastes were strewn with ruins; old bones and decaying refuse were flung about and picked over by the jackals, or the gipsies' dogs which now set up a furious barking as the strangers drew near. The gipsies' performing bears – tragic, mangy creatures – dragged at their chains, whining and snuffling uneasily. But the gipsies, sprawling among their rags, paid no heed and Edward breathed more freely.

They left these desolate outskirts of the city behind them and now entered a grove where the road petered out into a track. All around lay open country and they could hear the jackals yelping close by. Bursts of firing still sounded fitfully. Rosie leaned out of the palki, straining her eyes for a last glimpse of Delhi. She could distinguish the domes and minarets of the great mosque, the Musjid Jumma which she had so often passed beneath, going to take her pleasures at Baghmati's house. The mosque was silhouetted against a flickering copper-coloured sky. They were setting light to parts of the city . . . She wondered what was happening in Shäitanpura.

As the bullocks plodded on with their usual air of resignation, the palki slung between them rolled and jerked and the two women pitched from side to side, so that Florence was seldom without her smelling salts. They travelled by night, less to avoid the heat of the day, (for the nights were scarcely cooler), than to escape encounters which might be fatal. The country they passed through seemed quiet, but whether this was a pastoral calm, or the stillness of an animal waiting to spring, they could not tell, for they stayed aloof from the villages. During the fever hours of noon they lay sweating under the dense-leaved mango trees, or in thickets, the bullocks tethered nearby, while the camel, freed from its sinister burden, chewed mouthfuls of thorn, its long yellow teeth showing in a sneer of rage when it could not reach some particularly desirable branch.

All day that breathless hot wind peculiar to the country round Delhi puffed at them, furnace-like. They watched with envy the shining black bulk of water buffaloes wallowing in streams where, towards sunset, the villagers came down to bathe; the women, graceful, narrow-hipped creatures, waded in the shallows, their saris looped up between their legs to form a kind of draped pantaloon, as they pounded their washing on the stones, or fetched water in big brass pots. But although Rosie spoke longingly of paddling, none of the party dared approach the villagers. Only the bearers were safe to forage for food, a few handfuls of rice or a bowl of curds. Sometimes Edward rode out at dusk after small game, his marksmanship rather hampered by the long, old-fashioned flintlock his Persian disguise imposed. And sometimes, returning triumphant with snipe or wild kid, he would try to inveigle Florence deeper into the thickets, while the servants prepared their supper.

'But, Florence my love, don't you care for me anymore? After all, you are my wife. What is the matter?' Alas, India was the matter and Edward was to blame for bringing her there. Florence was embittered, unromantic. It was bad enough when he importuned her in those smelly French hotels, on their honeymoon – or in Cairo, or that stifling bungalow in Delhi . . . but now . . .

'Oh, Edward, not now, please . . . it's too hot . . . someone might see us . . . what about the cobras . . .? A hundred reasons to deny Edward what, in the flights of her novelette-fed imagination, she believed she longed to have offered another. Though even the glittering phantom of desire which the Rao Jagnabad once represented had now been reduced to shadowy proportions by the miseries of her present existence. So Edward, never very demanding,, would return self consciously to the servants squatting by the cooking pot, and Florence would follow to pick at the food and remark for the hundredth time that she hated eating with her fingers.

As they drew near to Agra, the bearers returned from scouting expeditions to tell of unrest and violence there too. The British were mewed up in Akbar's Red Fort. Some had barricaded themselves in the deserted city of Fathi-pur-Sikhri, said the villagers contemptuously. They could share its emptiness with the jackals and the scorpions that were the only living things left there; they could share it with its ghosts . . . When the time was ripe, they would be smoked out like rats and put to the sword. There was no hurry, they said voluptuously. It was good to have the Ferenghis at their mercy at last. The two Sikhs reported their mood sadly. It was not how all Indians felt, they said. Nevertheless, there were terrible dangers everywhere now. So when at last Edward saw the crimson turrets of Agra's Fort rising from the dusty plains, he dared not approach.

Now his story must change. He must choose some obscure place, farther ahead, in which to be burying the father-in-law. They must skirt the city by a wide detour and resume their route a night's march away. Florence, who had been sustained by thoughts of this nightmare journey being broken at Agra, of being once more among her own kind and recovering in civilized surroundings, now had an attack of hysterics, and to her surprise, was slapped by Rosie. But it pulled her together quicker than all Edward's solicitude. The discomforts of the journey had, for her, quite obscured its dangers. Since Edward took care to minimize his fears; and Rosie seemed as blithe as ever; and the bearers were fatalistic, whispering their uneasiness to their sahib alone – Florence had never properly grasped their peril. The fact that they were alive, unmolested, and reasonably well at the end of each day seemed to her less extraordinary than the fact that she had not been able to change her clothes or take a bath since leaving Delhi, or that Rosie, her maid, one of the lower classes, had slapped her.

After nearly three weeks of this journeying, which in spite of its dangers was above all tedious, they reached Azampur. It was a small British outpost, following the usual pattern: an Indian quarter, the original village, centred round the bazaars, had been elbowed aside by the cantonments. The Protestant church, its toy-like spire rising prim and incongruous beside great clumps of exotic vegetation, and the unassuming but solidly comfortable houses of the officers and their families now dominated the scene. Very little news of the mutiny had reached Azampur, though it was known that unrest was spreading. The villages around were quiet, but rumours of

Delhi's sack, of British unpreparedness, had fanned the flames everywhere. It was only a matter of time, said the commanding officer, before Azampur was infected.

Even so, the fugitives felt they had earned some repose, and at last were sleeping on real beds once more, enjoying real food – for so English preserved delicacies now appeared to them. Potted meats, tinned sausages and pickles were pressed on them and bottled porter seemed like nectar. There was no shortage of supplies at present, but the Colonel looked increasingly grim as native spies came in telling of disasters up and down the country. No man could say how long it would be before revolt took hold here too. The women and children of the station must be moved to safety. If they could undertake a four-hundred mile journey into Rajputana where the ruler of one small kingdom was known to be loyal to the British, they might be left in his care without anxiety. He was a sixteen-gun salute Maharaja, a most honourable man, said the Colonel; and his officers agreed. It was the only solution – the women must go.

Runners were dispatched to sound out the Maharaja in question and presently returned with a detachment of cavalry sent by the ruler to escort the memsahibs back to his territories without delay. The Maharaja was passionately loyal to England for a number of good reasons and was now convinced this was a God-given chance to prove his fidelity. In an illuminated address over which his Court scribes had laboured, (under threat of torture), to satisfy both the literary and artistic demands of their Lord and Master, he stated that the English ladies should be lodged in his own palace. Quarters in the zenana would be placed at their disposal and they should want for nothing. 'Their pillows shall be strewn with rose leaves and they shall walk on pearls,' he wrote. His servants would be theirs and his soldiers would protect them with their own lives. He – the Maharaja, the Glorious Sun of the Morning – would slay with his own sword – the tulwar of his mighty ancestors – the first person who harmed them in word or deed.

Hospitality could go no further. Thus encouraged, the Colonel ordered that the ladies of the station, twenty-three of them in all, should leave forthwith. Edward had decided to try and make his way to Oudh. If he could not reach his own post up country, he would head for Lucknow where it was believed the situation was serious, and they would be glad of any man who could hold a gun. Edward was a civilian, but he was a good shot and he knew the country and the languages. There must be something he could do there, he thought. What he did not know was that Lucknow was already a besieged city; inaccessible and ringed by baleful rebel armies. On the night of 30 May, while he was skirting Agra, the first shots had been exchanged. Now the British held out with heroic madness from the flimsy defences of the Residency.

Early in July the siege was to enter its most tragic phase. Even if a man got through to reinforce the defenders, he was another mouth to feed. There were scarcely enough rations left to keep the children alive and the wounded were dying as much from malnutrition as from lack of medical supplies.

But none of this was known as yet in Azampur, so by mid-June Edward set out, once more wearing the turban and atamsouk of the Persian merchant, and accompanied still by one of the bearers. The other, his mission accomplished, had vanished into the countryside. He wanted no part in the strife that was now beginning and was heading for his village south of the Sutlej. Edward took as much ammunition as the Colonel could spare him, and a lock of Florence's hair, which in both the giving and taking, they felt fulfilled the classic pattern of parting. Edward also slipped a copy of Plato, borrowed from the Chaplain, into his saddlebags. He had always liked to read the classics at breakfast, something – like breakfast, for that matter – which he had been obliged to forgo during their flight from Delhi. Now, riding east to battle, but unencumbered by the bullock palki and its burden, he remembered how the mornings had dragged by as they lay in the shade of the mango trees, plagued by insects, hunger, thirst, heat and fear. Even so, Florence and Rosie had contrived to prattle, little more intelligibly, he thought, than the monkeys swinging in the branches above them. He sighed. Perhaps after all he was not really suited to the married state. It left so little quiet for thinking, for reading. In the short while they had been married he had found Florence a disturbing presence. It was odd. She made no demands on either his intellect, or his senses, yet the mere fact that she was there was an encroachment. It would have been simpler, he thought, if she had distracted him more physically. He would not have resented that, for of course even the most intellectual men wish women to attach the same importance to their virility as they do themselves.

V

While Edward rode east, at peace with himself again, Florence and Rosie were among the little group of women and children setting out for the shelter of the Maharaja's palace, four hundred miles to the west in the fiery heart of Rajputana, where this ruler was said to live in particular splendour. The farewells were not as heart rending as they might have been, for no one had yet realized the full implications of the Mutiny. The ladies were certain everything would blow over soon. They thought the Colonel was unduly alarmist. Still, there were the children to think of. So, although clinging and tearful, they felt no extreme dangers could be threatening their husbands – while their husbands were profoundly relieved to think their wives and children would escape the horrors which they apprehended. It was the children who seemed to mind the most, for they were being torn from their playthings and their pets – kittens, squirrels in cages, and anxious-eyed dogs, whimpering, as well they might, for never again would they know affection, or care. The pet animals of that hour could seldom be saved – abandoned, turned loose, shot if they were lucky, lost, forgotten . . . They too were engulfed in the Mutiny's terrible tide.

The children, bawling inconsolably, were joined in their grief by their devoted ayahs, wailing and casting themselves on the ground. But at last order was restored and the children stowed into the tongas along with the carpet bags, or small bundles, which were all their mothers were permitted to take with them. A few of the older women rode with the children in tongas, but most of the party were mounted on ponies; the strong little beasts which had been the pride of the officers playing polo on the burnt-up grass beyond the cantonments.

All saddle horses must be kept for the garrison, said the Colonel, but their get-away must be as speedy as possible, said Risaldar Sadun Singh, the Maharaja's officer commanding the escort; ponies, mules – no matter, so long as they moved fast. There could be no lingering, nor he could not answer for their safety, by which the Colonel knew the revolt must be approaching Azampur.

On the morning of their departure, Risaldar Sadun Singh was cantering his horse up and down outside the Colonel's house before it was light. When the Colonel spoke a measured farewell address and wrung each woman's hand, the Risaldar was plainly in a fever to be off, while when he was further delayed by the Chaplain leading the whole station in a hymn, he flung himself out of the saddle and paced up and down, fuming. But at last they were moving. The drivers flourished their whips and the tongas rattled out of the compound followed by the women, Amazonian figures in riding habits or pinned-up skirts, their bonnets veiled in dark green or blue muslin. The cavalry escort pranced round them kicking up clouds of pink dust and bringing up the rear – his horse fretting as impatiently as its rider – was Risaldar Sadun Singh.

Rosie eyed him attentively and tried to edge her pony nearer. He was a dashing figure in splendid garments which recalled the Rao to both Florence and Rosie. Florence felt again a rush of the old shame and longing. Oh, would she never be able to forget the whole hateful episode? But Rosie, seeing that the dagger Sadun Singh wore at his waist had a handle fashioned like a horse's head, with flashing ruby eyes, recalled that it was similar to the one the Rao Jagnabad had flung down when he seized her in his arms. She settled herself more comfortably in her saddle to re-live the whole episode yet again. She never wanted to forget a moment of it.

The Risaldar Sadun Singh kept them moving at a fast pace. Except for a respite during the hottest part of the day, they lived in a perpetual dust cloud, a dimension of dust which choked them, gritted their eyes, and covered them with a greyish film till the women appeared a spectral band mounted on phantom horses passing across the vivid land. It was as if this Indian dust had a life of its own and differentiated between Indians and strangers, settling more heavily on the interloping Ferenghis, as if to oppress them, whereas it scarcely filmed the brown faces, or dimmed the brilliant turbans of the Risaldar's troop.

Sometimes, during the noonday halt, sheltering under the banyan trees, or in the shade of a deserted temple, they were surrounded by armies of monkeys which would appear from nowhere, rushing, grimacing, scuttling hordes with pleading eyes, reaching up with soft-skinned little black hands that could snatch a chupatty from a wailing child, or claw angrily at the soldiers who drove them off half-heartedly. The monkeys were sacred, they said, when some of the ladies complained. Was not the great God Hanuman of their kind? No Hindu would raise his hand against the monkey people.

Florence sat in the shade of a crumbling doorway, watching the big, grey-maned, black-faced creatures running frieze-like along the top of a wall, tiny wizened babies clinging upside down to their mothers' bellies.

'Ugly little things,' she said and closed her eyes. She was feeling sick again, and hoped that nothing unfortunate had happened . . . that she was not . . . not expecting. It really was too inconsiderate of Edward . . . and during the journey from Delhi too, with Rosie and the bearers always somewhere about. And then, that horrible corpse – one could scarcely be expected to feel romantic in such circumstances. But Edward could be very tactless at times. When she'd told him she really couldn't – not with that dreadfully evident body close by – he had laughed quite cynically and said something about the quick and the dead which she had not understood. Really, sometimes she did not understand Edward at all. He had been most pressing that evening. Yet she thought she'd made it quite clear to him on their honeymoon that she didn't care for that sort of thing . . . The possibility of such a calamity overtaking her here and now was appalling. She no longer thought of children as a wife's first duty, however trying. Now she simply prayed to get out of India as soon as possible. Nothing must keep her here, not even her marriage to Edward.

She no longer saw the monkeys, or the frescoed walls of the abandoned palace where they were. She no longer saw the painted figures with which it was decorated – turbaned warriors, or girls on rooftops, playing the sita or gazing down on their suitors from the selfsame carved lattices below which the cavalcade now rested; all faded. In their place, Florence saw Bogwood Hall, its façade grey in the slanting rain, the boles of the beech trees glistening black, the bare branches dripping. How cool and safe it looked. There was her bedroom window with its holland blind and there was Mama's room and the conservatory. Had she ever thought it dull? Her ready tears welled up again and spilled down, making runnels through the dust and sweat which caked her cheeks.

'I want to go home,' she sobbed despairingly.

Great cry baby, thought Rosie, who had never had a home worth calling such, and therefore did not understand homesickness. But the other ladies did and they gathered round, patting and sympathetic. They would like to have been more friendly with Florence, but she kept herself rather aloof. She was a newcomer to them, as to India, and she did not seem to gather any resilience, as they had learned to do. Poor little Mrs Mulgrove, they said, so delicate, she never ought to have come out, the climate is too much for her altogether. But she was a Viscount's daughter, so they made allowances when they thought she gave herself airs, or kept Rosie waiting on her hand and foot. None of them had brought out European maids and now, deprived of the services of their numerous native servants, they were obliged to fend for themselves, something most of them had done, uncomplainingly, in England, but which life in India had taught them to regard as a disastrous loss of face.

Rosie they mistrusted from the start. She was a sly baggage. You had only to see the way she looked at the soldiers – blacks, too – to know she was up to no good. Why on earth had the Mulgroves brought her out with them? Still, she seemed good-natured enough and they were not above accepting her offer to wash their linen for them, although they were all outraged when she presented them with a laundry bill – little enough, but then, nothing for nothing, as Rosie said pleasantly in answer to their pinched looks. As to Mrs Mulgrove, she didn't seem able to say boo to a goose, let alone control her maidservant, so Rosie was allowed to collect the money she had earned. She spent it all at the next village buying sticky, unhealthy-looking sweets for the children and nuts for the monkeys, feeding them in alternate handfuls, first an ape, then a toddler, without any regard for hygienic principles until the human mothers, seeing their offspring jostled by apes, snatched them away from this degrading proximity, leaving the simian families to their treat.

If the memsahibs regarded Rosie as an outcast, she did not seem to notice, or care. She thought them a milk-and-water lot, stuck up and mean. But there it was. For the present they must all be together, or at least in the same cavalcade. So when they camped for the night, or rested at noon, she settled herself a little beyond their circle. Now, as they sheltered from the implacable midday sun, while Florence sat fanning herself in the shade of the ruined palace, Rosie was flung down beneath a jacaranda tree, on her outspread burqa which made a most useful travelling cloak. Besides, it was a souvenir. She had insisted on keeping it when she and Florence had been fitted out with European clothes by the ladies of Azampur. As Edward's wife, Florence had been given a very pretty pearl-grey silk, while Rosie had been allotted a suitably work-a-day cotton. But both of them were clogged by a number of frilled petticoats and the long lace-edged linen drawers then worn by every European woman, whatever her station in life.

Rosie was staring up at the deep blue sky. It looked violet between the purple clusters of the jacaranda. A purple tree and a violet sky . . . But she was getting used to the improbabilities of India. Behind rose a burnt scrub hillside, orange in the sunlight. It was a mountainous slope, jagged with rocks, and Rosie, trying to follow the soldiers' talk, thought they were saying it was tiger country. She kept this disquieting information to herself. No good alarming Miss Florence – she and all the rest of the ladies carried on so when they were upset. Besides, it would never do if Miss Florence or any of the others found out how much of the Hindu lingo she understood. They might ask awkward questions. Shäitanpura and all she'd learned there was best kept to herself. It might come in handy later, you could never tell. Still, it was funny how quick she'd been to pick up that foreign talk. Just as if it was meant to be.

Tiger country! She thought with violent longing of Jagnabad, the Nine Tiger Man, with his ruthless hunter's face. He would have been off hunting them now, bringing back their tawny skins proudly, to lay them at her feet . . . She impatiently brushed aside the possibility of present dangers. After all, there were a dozen armed men with them – though privately Rosie thought them a good-for-nothing crew; by which she meant they never so much as glanced in her direction, treating her with an impersonal deference not at all to her liking. But the men knew they were answerable with their own lives for the safe-conduct of every one of these memsahibs. Even if they had found any of them pleasing, (and to most Indians, light hair and eyes were considered both unattractive and unlucky), they would not have dared approach them. These were guests of their ruler, the Maharaja. So they primed their guns, alert for dangers and Rosie's inviting glances went unacknowledged.

As they moved west, the beauty of the lovely countryside seemed to gather momentum, revealing more and more loveliness. Wide valleys were watered by streams and ringed by distant mountains. Great trees shaded the still splendid ruins of palaces and ancient temples, extraordinarily carved, where the people came to adorn their various gods with garlands of marigolds and jasmine. In spite of the intense heat, it was a green and flowering land of abundance. The cavalcade moved through it with a dream-like sense of unreality, for it was unlike anything they had known in the arid central plains. Now, too, they seemed to have entered a kingdom of birds, moving beneath a canopy of winged creatures which darted, perched, fluttered, trilled and shrieked above them. Along the roofs of the villages the peacocks lorded it, rustling their quills as they strutted. Parakeets and little scarlet-and-yellow birds flashed in the sunlight, long-necked 'snake-birds' swayed among the leaves, and the doves cooed, monotonously affectionate. The more tonic note of the mynah birds followed them as the birds themselves, hopping from branch to branch, watched them with their sharp golden eyes and uttered piercing whistle calls, as if wishing to communicate some urgent information. Large turquoise-winged birds preened among the stubble, or perched in the ever shivering silvery leaves of the holy peepul trees, their plumage gaudy among the scraps of rag which pious villagers hung there, prayer offerings to the sacred tree, reminders to some god that even here, in this green and easy kingdom, the people suffered and craved godly aid.

Above, bending the highest treetops with their weight, perched obscene-looking vultures, great bag-like forms gorged on filth and eyeing the refuse-strewn lanes for more. Sometimes they would plunge earthwards, malevolent and intent, fastening on some dying creature so that the ladies broke into a gallop to put distance between themselves and the merciless, inescapable face of nature, here in India. Even in this rich and pastoral scene, where the cattle were sleek and the people at ease, it was better not to think about the condition of domestic animals, for which it appeared neither nature nor man had made provision.

Rosie, who was fond of animals but whose knowledge of Hindu religions was sketchy, believed that Ganesh, her favourite, the elephant-headed god with his little friend the rat Vahan, was probably the god who concerned himself most over the animals. Looking at his image, with his benign elephant's head and his chubby arms and legs, she thought he seemed a kindly, approachable sort of deity. Sometimes, unobserved, she would contrive to leave a handful of flowers before his shrine, offering up a prayer for a litter of starving puppies, or a maltreated cat. Heathen Gods! Look out, my girl, she thought, catching herself addressing a particularly heartfelt prayer to him on behalf of an injured parrot pining in a cage so small it could not even shuffle round. No, it was better not to think about the animals.

The people – that was different; hereabouts, anyhow. They reflected the wellbeing of their countryside. The women, carrying their brass water jars to and from the wells, were beautiful and sensuous in their distinctive Rajput dress, the gathered, very full, bell-shaped skirts of orange, rose, scarlet or lemon muslin swirling above their braceleted ankles, their head veils interwoven with kincob, metal thread, giving them an air of almost theatrical allure. They reminded Rosie of the nautch girls she had watched in Shäitanpura. But these women were Rajputs – a race apart, fiery and proud.

'Rajputana! My land, my people!' said Sadun Singh with pride, seeing admiration on the faces of his charges. Florence remembered that the Rao Jagnabad was said to be a Rajput. Edward had told her they were a warrior race, the prototype of medieval chivalry. In defeat, he said, the women ran on the swords their men held steady for them, rather than suffer dishonour. How could she have demeaned herself writing to him like that! What must he have thought of her? Recalling her rebuff, her eyes filled with tears of mortification.

Whatever is she crying about now, Rosie wondered. She was well aware that parting from Mr Edward had not greatly grieved her young mistress. She supposed Florence was homesick again. The Rao was never mentioned between them and she had no way of knowing that Florence, like herself, had never forgotten the Nine Tiger Man.

They were nearing their destination, said the Risaldar Sadun Singh. They would be at the Palace by evening. Suddenly, each woman began in her own mind to primp. At noon there was a great deal of agitation as crumpled dresses were smoothed, bonnet-ribbons retied and the whole camp reeked of *eau de Cologne*. Hairpins and bottles of Macassar oil were greatly in demand, the ladies braiding, pinning and arranging one another with mutual solicitude. Florence contented herself with fastening her collar by a fine Greek intaglio brooch which Edward had bought for her in Alexandria. Rosie, having no other resources, emptied a small phial of attar of roses over herself. But then, she had learned how potent an appeal strong perfumes made to Eastern men. She had been saving the phial, a pretty little pink glass affair daubed with gold, a relic of her purchases in the Chandni Chowk, for some special occasion. Their arrival at the Palace, she felt, was such.

All that afternoon the road climbed steeply. Volcanic, cone-shaped hills, each one crowned by a little fort, guarded the passes. Between these outposts ran crenellated pink stone walls which followed the contours of the land uncompromisingly, plunging into ravines and straddling the crags. Now the women found themselves on the crest of a hill looking down over a chain of lakes ringed with palm-tufted shores where domed and pinnacled pavilions were reflected in the satiny water. From the centre of the largest lake an island of white marble glowed like some gigantic pearl. It was the most beautiful landscape any of the travellers had ever seen. Even Florence forgot to pine for

Bogwood in the rain. As they gazed, there was a rush of wings overhead and a green cloud of parakeets flew out across the lake towards the island, circling and dipping in flashes of emerald light as they sped into the last low beams of the sun.

The Risaldar raised his whip and pointed to a vast expanse of pinnacled rooftops lying immediately below them. This, he said, was the Palace, and here, the Maharaja would receive them. More primping, more dabs of *eau de Cologne*, more last-minute instructions to the children to be quiet, not to fidget; to curtsy properly. Some of them, over-excited now, had to be hurried off into the bushes, unbuttoned and rebuttoned again, while their escort waited patiently. All the mothers, and even the unmaternal Florence, had realized from the start of the journey how loving, how gentle, the soldiers were with the children. All of them, including the dashing Risaldar, displayed the utmost patience with their little charges, taking them up on their saddles for a gallop, dandling them, telling them marvellous stories and calming their fears. Like born nannies, thought Rosie, rather touched by this display of tenderness, which, had she known it, was an integral part of the Hindu nature, along with the ruthless ferocity of which, now, many British were aware for the first time.

They rode down through the narrow, steep streets of the town where dusk was falling fast, where the lamplit booths glowed and the people gathered in the doorways to stare curiously at the newcomers. Ferenghis, said the soldiers, memsahibs for the Maharaja. But the townspeople, seeing the dusty haggard faces, thought their Maharaja would have done better to choose local beauties. And beauties there were, in abundance. Even on this brief descent through the town, the ladies could see how fine-looking were these people, young or old, man or woman. The men wore their beards brushed upwards and outwards as the Rao Jagnabad had done. Most of them carried curved swords and round steel-bossed shields were slung across their shoulders, giving each man a martial air.

Even the mahouts, splashing naked in the shallows where the gigantic elephants lolled and trumpeted at their evening bath, seemed a military elite.

It was this warrior kingdom which now offered sanctuary to the memsahibs.

At last they reached the outer courtyard of the Palace and were led through vast halls, across long galleries, beneath marble archways lit by crystal chandeliers which reminded Florence of Stafford House, but where, in place of the flunkeys in their knee-breeches and powdered wigs, fierce, sullen-looking Palace retainers crouched, chewing betel nut. Or where guards with long spears sprang forward to bar their way, until, orders issuing from further infinite perspectives of fountained courts, they were at last admitted to the Diwan-i-Khaus, a pillared hall of audience, its marble walls inlaid with precious stones – lapis lazuli, malachite and mirrors all glittering in the lamplight.

Here the Maharaja was revealed, seated on a silver throne supported by gilded lions, an umbrella of state held over his head and surrounded by a number of sumptuously dressed courtiers and statesmen. As if to point up the fact that such majesty as his needed no added splendour, he was dressed in a rather grubby creased silk coat, where food stains were apparent beside the enormous plastron of diamonds which cascaded over his great belly, flashing as he heaved. Above his bristling white beard and moustachios, his eyes were brown and benign. He shot his short legs out from under his belly as if to rise, signal mark of esteem from such a personage – and then, having conveyed the measure of his regard, he fell back, panting alarmingly.

The memsahibs sank to the floor, curtsying their respect and gratitude, while the Maharaja struggled to regain his breath. At last he spoke in good English, pronouncing each word carefully, rolling it round his tongue along with the betel nut he was chewing, which revealed a vivid crimson lining to his mouth.

'Your troubles have passed,' he told them. 'Your husbands and fathers are as my brothers. I have sworn no harm shall befall you here. For greater safety you will be lodged on my island – on the Rani's island, home of my revered grandmother.' He waved a pudgy, heavily-ringed hand to where, beyond the arched verandahs, they could see the lake stretching away, dark and mysterious, under a rising moon.

'And let it be known,' he continued, turning on his Court, suddenly a figure of awful wrath, 'that he who harms a hair of the head of these, my honoured guests, shall answer to me with his life. My own sword – the sword of my ancestors – shall cut him down.'

Clutching this sword, he fell back panting on the pearl-tasselled bolsters which supported him. His little legs dangled and one embroidered slipper fell to the ground. Rosie noticed that each stumpy brown toe was ringed with precious stones.

His attendants hurried forward, one to replace the slipper, the next to fan him with a great sheaf of peacock feathers, the morchel, a royal prerogative, like the umbrella of Majesty. The audience was at an end. Overawed, the travellers filed out.

At the marble steps of the palace landing stage, the boatmen were manoeuvring a state barge. It was strangely shaped, with a roofed pavilion and a high curved prow in the form of a gigantic prancing horse. The children had been piled on board and the ladies were now making a great to do, bunching up their skirts and uttering little shrieks as the guards picked them up and slung them over to the boatmen. Rosie and Florence were among the last to go, when there was a sudden stir among the guards. A horseman, his jewelled turban flashing in the moonlight and followed by a small retinue, had ridden at a gallop right into the palace precincts. Surrounded by bowing servitors, he flung the reins to one and strode across the courtyard towards the inner labyrinths. On his wrist he carried a sahin falcon on a jewelled leash. He was clearly a person of consequence. One of their bigwigs, thought Rosie, watching him, and wondering what sort of people they would find on the island.

But the rider, seeing the royal barge beside the steps and the knot of European women on board, turned back and came closer. Taking a lantern from one of the watermen he held it aloft, the better to see what strange fish had been washed up on the lakeside. He was a tall, powerful figure and the lamplight sculpted his dark face in bold relief. It was the face of a hunter. At the same moment both Florence and Rosie recognized the Rao Jagnabad – the Nine Tiger Man – their hearts' desire.

VI

The boatmen pulled towards the Rani's island, their gilded oars slicing rhythmically into the still dark water where the reflections of a few stars were netted in the ripples. As the lighted façade of the Palace dwindled, the sounds of the surrounding town faded. Clanging portals, the clash and clatter of the sentries' arms and distant music – flute, sita and drumbeat – grew fainter and were lost. A curious silence now fell over the boatload of women. They became oppressed, apprehensive even, in spite of the assurances of their husbands and the stately welcome of the Maharaja. They strained their eyes into the darkness to make out the island which was to shelter them. Slowly, its outline was emerging from the lake, a confused mass of tall trees, shadowy domes and pinnacles rising sheer from the water. But all was darkness. There were no lights, no sounds, no signs of life; it might have been a desert isle. As they peered ahead, a bobbing firefly light suddenly appeared threading its way through the thickets, coming and going in the blackness until it stopped at the water's edge, shining feebly over a flight of steps beside which the boatmen were now making fast. Along each side of these steps, dimly outlined in the starlight, was a row of life-size stone elephants, their trunks raised in the pachyderm's traditional salute. They loomed over the landing stage like gigantic watchdogs, seeming to challenge rather than welcome any human being setting foot in this domain of silence; this animal kingdom given over to the jungle and its creatures. The women felt slighted, neglected. Stone beasts were poor substitutes for a reception committee . . . for some representatives of the Maharaja's household, at least. They were a spoiled lot and had been accustomed to a great deal of deference from 'the natives' – even the princes.

However, times had changed. They must be thankful they were still alive . . . Their snapping nerves found relief in speaking sharply to the children who had at once rushed towards the elephants, and were now trying to clamber over them swinging from the tusks.

'Alfred! Come down this minute! You know Papa has told you time and again not to go near the idols.'

Elephants! I'll give you elephants!' then came the sound of a slap in the darkness.

'Louisa, I'm ashamed of you, climbing about like that. You're not a boy!'

Bawling and whining, the children were brought to heel while their mothers stood huddled together in increasing uneasiness.

Florence and Rosie were silent. Each was preoccupied with her own thoughts, which were, had they known it, identical. The sudden apparition of the Rao had left each of them stunned. Neither knew if the other had recognized him, nor did they know if he had recognized them, for after staring long and silently, he had turned on his heel and entered the Palace without a backward glance. Neither woman spoke of this hallucinatory moment. Both their hearts were still beating wildly, for both were, once again, overcome by the force of their emotions. Florence, agitated and romantic, believed he had picked her out from the rest of the party, was sure his long dark eyes had perceived her, but now she did not know whether she longed for him, or dreaded the renewal of the torments he had roused. Rosie simply determined that if she did not see him on the island, soon, she would have to get back to the mainland and look for him there.

As the women stood faltering on the steps of the Rani's island, chiding their children and wondering what to do next, the firefly light moved closer and they saw it was a lantern held in the wavering hand of a very old man, a phantom figure, followed by another phantom, haglike and ancient. They were an odd-looking pair, quite unlike anyone Florence or Rosie had seen since their arrival in India. Their faces were flat, wrinkled and yellow and their narrow eyes were steeply slanted. Both wore long padded coats and were decked out in huge copper and turquoise ornaments. They wore curiously shaped heavy felt boots with upturned toes and the four corners of the old woman's head-dress also curved up, each corner being hung with little bells, like the Chinese pagoda in the park at Bogwood, thought Florence wearily, surprised that she still had strength to notice anything.

These two decrepit creatures watched in silence as the boatmen raised their oars in a last salute and were swallowed up in the night, returning to the mainland. Then, still in silence, with pantomime beckonings and shuffling steps, they conducted the newcomers along a narrow path, little more than a clearing in the jungle, which gave abruptly on to the forecourt of a small but seemingly splendid palace – no doubt that of the Rani after whom the island was named. Silhouetted against the starry sky, domes and pavilions soared above them. Across the marble courtyard ran a watercourse, fed by a central fountain where the reflected stars shivered into prisms of light as a faint orange-scented breeze ruffled the surface of the pool. Taking the lantern from the old man, the crone motioned the ladies inside the palace. Fearfully, they passed under a high, brass-spiked doorway and followed her into further realms of shadowy silence. Even the children were quiet now and Rosie caught herself walking on tiptoe.

They found themselves in a large domed hall, surrounded by pillared alcoves, and cooled by windows open on to the night and the jungle. The crone lit another, larger lantern. Suddenly the room sprang to life around them. A thousand, thousand pinpoints of light glittered and sparked from the myriads of mirror fragments with which walls and ceiling were inlaid. These were set in a fine tracery of greyish plaster and carved wood, so that it seemed as if a million diamonds were caught up in a million more spiders' webs. The whole room shimmered, light sparking in each fragment when the old woman moved the lantern. As the newcomers gazed spellbound at this strange firmament, she grinned and mumbled and lit a taper which she waved aloft, pointing upwards with her grubby, henna-stained old hand, so that they saw a thousand more will-o'-the-wisp lights flitting about the lofty dome. The children, enchanted and over excited, began trying to catch the prisms that flashed from the few pieces of furniture, low tables and throne-like seats that were mirror-encrusted like all the rest.

In this glittering twilight, the women stood drooping, eyeing one another's drawn faces and whispering fearfully, for such was the atmosphere which this place exuded. For all its splendours and exotic beauty, it was forbidding. Or did it perhaps only manifest its hostility towards these forlorn figures because they were so clearly not on pleasure bent? Perhaps, its extravagance having been the setting for so many equally extravagant *voluptés*, the new arrivals struck an offensively alien and drab note, of which the spirit of the place, the *genius loci*, was aware, and resented, like the stone elephants on the landing stage.

The women whispered among themselves and the sound echoed round the shimmering ceiling. Where did they sleep? What did they eat? Who was to look after them? Vain questionings. The old woman appeared not to hear when they spoke, or even shouted, in their basic Hindustani. Florence struggled to recall the few phrases she had mastered from Murray's *Phrase Book*. 'Keep the punkahs going all night!' . . . 'Has any sick person slept in this bed lately?' (Useful for *dâk* bungalow travel, Edward had said, when she remarked its sinister implications.) Oh Edward! Oh Mama! Oh India! dreadful, dirty, alarming India.

Now the crone was dragging in a number of cushions and padded cotton quilts which she piled in the centre of the hall. Her gestures told them that here was their bedding and here they must sleep. Food? Drink? The privy? She paid no heed to their demands. The whole party was now suffering acutely from thirst. One by one, the ladies ordered water to be brought immediately. But the old woman simply went on stacking up the cushions, the old man tripping over them. Rosie disliked the memsahibs' habitually arrogant tones and now tried out her own halting but more colloquial Hindustani. She had remarked that among themselves the Indians were most polite in their address to even the lowliest. Sweepers or scavengers were 'Mehtar – Prince!' 'Hey! Maharaj!' shouted the Risaldar Sadun Singh when some drowsy bullock-cart driver obstructed the road.

'O man of Paradise, bring water!' Rosie now contrived, employing, however haltingly, the formula she had so often heard Mother Baghmati's porters use, calling the *bhistis* or water carriers of Shäitanpura. The assembled ladies looked surprised at this flowery approach.

'Water, bring water, O man of Paradise!' She repeated the formula hopefully, but there was no response. At last, by dint of pantomiming their thirst, several large brass jars of rather brackish water were obtained and the old hag stumbled in with an enormous silver platter, its border studded with rubies, its centre piled with leathery chupatties. This mixture of luxury and the barest necessities, magnificence beside squalor, was everywhere apparent on the island. It was a concentration of the same juxtapositions found throughout India, particularly in those regions where what the British termed their refining and civilizing influence had not been imposed. The children fell on the food, but most of their mothers were now too overcome with fatigue and anxiety to eat anything. The old couple had bid them good night in some sort of cackling gabble, salaamed, and shuffled out of sight before anyone thought to try and get them to close the shutters. The windows gaped wide on to the night and there were no panes of glass to combat either the assaults of mosquitoes, or possibly wild animals. But sleep overcame fear. They had started before dawn. The Risaldar Sadun Singh had pressed on, allowing them no halt at noon that day, so great was his impatience to render his charges to the Maharaja. They had been travelling for more than eighteen hours and now kicked off their shoes and slept where they fell, in careless heaps, among the splendours of the Rajput sanctuary.

Yet, exhausted as they were, neither Rosie nor Florence, lying under a shared quilt, closed their eyes without evoking the Rao Jagnabad's tormenting image. And to both, lying there side by side, the one pale and wan like a Gothic effigy on a tomb, the other pink and rounded like a baroque angel, he reappeared, conjured by the strength of their desires, to possess them in that other world of sleep as he possessed them, either in the spirit or the flesh, when awake.

The morning light roused Rosie early. It streamed in golden and pure, through the openings of each alcove. Beyond, the glowing emerald depths of the jungle and overgrown gardens were alive with green parakeets, while the piercing shrieks of the mynah birds sounded above all the chittering and scuffling of monkeys and squirrels, tree mice, bandicoots and the other wild creatures which, she guessed correctly, thronged the island. Rosie looked around her at the sleepers. They lay there turning uneasily in their sleep. Some of the children had adenoids and slept with their mouths open. Florence looked paper pale, her hair lying limp around her, and she was muttering in her sleep. Going down with another of her feverish attacks, thought Rosie with exasperation. She had come out as Florence's maid, not her nurse. Rosie detested illness, nursing and particularly 'delicacy', a state the ladies often discussed in detail. 'Another of my sick-headaches', 'one of my bad days', 'just another of my giddy attacks', they would say, prefixing the symptom with a possessive pronoun. *Delicacy*, Rosie had observed with scorn, was a state peculiar to the rich. Never the poor – they were too busy; they were well, or ill; they lived, or died – but they were not delicate.

Rosie slid out from under the coverlet, found her shoes and crept towards the door, stepping quietly over the sleepers. Beside the brass nail-studded entrance she noticed a narrow stairway. She thought it might be a good idea to explore and to acquaint herself better with her surroundings, before the others awoke. She climbed the stairs and found herself on the sort of roof terrace which is typical of every Indian dwelling, in varying degrees of splendour, or decay. This terrace, like the rest of the palace, was a mixture of both. Flowerpots which had once contained sweet-smelling plants lay overturned and dried up. Tattered silk cushions, their embroideries faded, were strewn about the floor of a little gold-roofed pavilion that hung out over the treetops. The delicately fretted marble lattices and balustrades were chipped. On a step, someone, long ago, had left a bowl of fruit. Now it was filled with dust and dead insects and the fruits were withered, blackened stones. At one side of the terrace hung a swing – an elaborate silver swing, chased and ornate, and similar to the one which the Rao had brought to Bogwood. While that one had been polished and gleaming, this one was blackened and dull and hung askew. But it was still a charming object. Rosie thought she would like to clean it up and swing in it in the cool of the evening. Yes, that's what she'd do.

A small ornamental fountain was the centrepiece of the terrace rooftop, but now it was dried up; the marble basin cracked and stained. In it, a pair of scorpions were mating angrily. Rosie watched them, repelled and fascinated by the ritual. She was glad to turn away, to look across the treetops that surrounded the palace like a green sea stretching away to the lake lying satin-smooth and blue, edged with fringed palms and sandy shores. In the morning light every tuft of vegetation, every fold of the hills, had the stillness and clarity which reminded Rosie of those views she used to peer at in the wonderful stereopticon machine which had been one of Miss Florence's treasures at Bogwood. The shores merged with the jungles, the jungles with the wild hills; and they with the volcanic, cone-shaped peaks beyond. Nowhere was there a sign of human habitation. North, south, west, no village, no fisherman's hut, no temple – nothing broke the stillness, the loneliness, of this paradisiacal scene.

But turning eastwards, from where the sun was climbing fast, Rosie could see the Maharaja's palace, gleaming and golden, surrounded by clusters of smaller buildings descending to the water's edge, broken here and there by the glint of a gilded temple, or the dark mass of a gigantic banyan tree. It was very far away: five or six miles away across the lake, Rosie reckoned. She began to wonder how she would get back there. Best bribe the boatman, she thought. Then the thought struck her: were there any boatmen here to be bribed? From the rooftop, the Rani's island looked as deserted as the farthest shores. Was it possible they had been dumped here, deliberately, to die? She shook off such a calamitous thought. No doubt the Maharaja's officers would be coming across this morning to install them more comfortably. There must be someone who would be responsible for them, to whom they could speak. Someone, she thought, who would be able to tell her what the Rao Jagnabad was doing at the palace.

Across to the south, halfway over the lake, Rosie now noticed a tiny islet, a mere hump of sand, with two tall palm trees sprouting from it, round which numerous enormous birds were circling and dipping, alighting to paddle and peck along the miniature shore. These were cranes, 'adjutant birds', ibis, cormorants and pelicans, had she known it, but there was no one to explain Indian wildlife since Mr Edward had gone. Rosie thought she saw a boat lying up on the tiny strand . . . it was becoming difficult to make anything out clearly, for early as it was, a shimmering heat haze had already settled over the water, blurring her vision. Anyhow, if there was a boat, then there must be boatmen, she reflected; and suddenly felt both cheerful and hungry. She was happy here, in this violent land. Every day, when the rest of the Englishwomen were complaining, she drew farther away from them and nearer to this strange East in which she never felt a stranger.

She gazed round again ecstatically, hugging the beautiful scene to her. I must have a look at it in my magic ring, she thought, diving in her pocket for the Hindu marriage ring which her Eurasian lover had bought for her in the silver markets of the Chandni Chowk. Rosie had known few possessions in her life. Even in childhood she had been without toys. This little Indian bauble was to her both a toy and a magical treasure. She liked to peer at each tiny scene it reflected, for it seemed to give back an even more fabulous Indian world – a microcosm of this marvellous East; diminished, yet heightened in intensity. Somehow it had a look of those tiny objects which she used to discover baked into the centre of the sugarsticks and humbugs that were doled out at the orphanage at Christmas. Each bite revealed a miniature world for sweet tooths – a little man, a little house, a little flower, each enclosed in a sugary sphere of its own. It was thus that the island appeared to her now, improbable, remote and infinitely desirable.

Even out of the looking glass it still appeared too small to be real. Why, it must be almost as small as that mound where the ducks lived in the middle of the village pond at home, she thought. She had a sudden vision of the mud and the weedy scum that filmed its surface; duckweed, they called it – funny she should remember that now. The pond was always choked with decaying leaves and greyish glutinous masses of frogspawn swayed listlessly against its edge. She used to go there to hunt for tadpoles as a child. She shivered, remembering the blustery cold of an English spring. She had never liked being out of doors in England. She recalled some very depressing outings across the fields with William, on their evening off, when he would lead her to a sodden haystack, there to tumble, while the sad Sunday bells clanged for evensong.

But here – a sudden surge of warmth and happiness swept

over her – here it was different. Here, there was the sun and the colours and the flowers – and the Rao Jagnabad. She would wish him to her side. Rosie had convinced herself that her ring possessed magic properties and that if she wished hard enough, as the brides must have done, summoning their bridegrooms to them, whatever or whoever she wanted would one day materialize. One day, looking into it, she would see the Rao over her shoulder, and turning, find him there – conjured up by the force of her love. Hadn't she spent many hours wishing him to her side in Shäitanpura, and again on the flight from Delhi? She kept the ring hidden, but in secret she had so often stared into its winking eye, wishing, wishing him into her arms. And then, last night, when suddenly he had ridden into the Maharaja's courtyard, wasn't that proof? He had been summoned – he had come!

Now she would wish him here beside her on the Rani's island. Or better still, she'd wish them alone together on the bird islet, away from the ladies. She held up the ring, shifting it till she caught the islet in the tiny circle of mirror. It lay there, basking and shimmering in the heat haze. She began to form her wish. A picnic there – just us – in the cool of the evening, that would be perfect, she thought dreamily. Peering again into the ring she noticed that the boat was now gone. 'That's odd,' she said, speaking aloud in her surprise. 'Someone must have been there all the time.' But no boat was to be seen anywhere on the expanses of the lake. They must have rowed round to the other side of the island while I wasn't looking, she decided. And also decided she must get hold of a boat herself, and row over to explore the islet, and the shores beyond.

Rosie was contented by nature, inventing and enjoying all kinds of treats, planning her pleasures with a childish enjoyment sometimes quite at variance with the pleasures involved. It might be a new ribbon for her cap, dripping toast for tea, or some strange silent wooing in the curtained rooms at Baghmati's establishment. Or as now, it might be planning to explore the lakeside. But at this moment she was going to enjoy her breakfast – if she could get any. She skipped down the narrow stairway beaming, to find the hall full of ladies, awakening in various degrees of irritability. Florence was thoroughly vexed.

'Goodness me! Rosie, wherever have you been? You gave me such a fright! We thought something must have happened to you. What were you thinking of, going off like that.' The scoldings left no place for Rosie's rapturous descriptions of the scenery, which in any case was the last thing the ladies wished to hear about. They crowded round anxiously. Who had she seen? What were they to eat? What were they to do next?

'Make the best of it, I suppose,' replied Rosie rather tartly, for she was sharp set and saw no sign of breakfast. She thought longingly of the porridge and cold pork of the servants' hall breakfasts at Bogwood.

But making the best of it was precisely what the ladies could not do. As time went by, each day the same as the next, a succeeding pattern of sunrise, sunset and nightfall, the hours only punctuated by sparse meals brought by the old woman, they began to take stock of their plight. They were no longer in actual danger. Indeed, they were only too far removed from the mainland. They were fed and lodged, but entirely alone. No boat called, no messages reached them, as if the stone elephants, having once admitted them to the island, now kept guard over them with an excessive zeal. No living soul inhabited the island, save the two aged spectres, who must be from Nepal, said one of the ladies who had visited the Tibetan borderlands. In any case, it was plain there could be no communication with them. They lived in an abandoned cage which had been part of the palace menagerie. Its bars were rusted, its doors swung open and a rank odour hung about it. The phantoms shared their unsavoury quarters with several shaggy black goats which strayed about in the garbage by which it was surrounded.

The ladies always hoped their own food was not prepared

here, but it did no good to inquire too closely. The old creatures were suspicious and sly. They did not like being observed and would mutter angrily and shuffle off into the jungle. They had a remarkable way of vanishing. Then the ladies felt entirely abandoned. It was wiser not to alienate them and to accept unquestioningly whatever attentions they were accorded.

Their food was monotonous: chupatties, sometimes rice, dal, or unnameable curries fried in rancid oil. But there were egg plants, green peppers and the fruits – the many sumptuous fruits which grew everywhere. Meat or fish never appeared and they came to the conclusion that the island must have been well stocked with flour and rice and oil in anticipation of their arrival, but that otherwise it had been decreed by the Maharaja that they must live off the resources of the place, and that their safety could only be absolute if nobody from the mainland ever approached the island. Florence listened to their views in silence and felt thankful that the matter was taken out of her hands – that she was not going to have to face a possible meeting with the Rao Jagnabad. Rosie also listened. Remembering the Nine Tiger Man, she thought they were paying too high a price for safety.

The children soon settled to their new life, plunging shrieking through the green jungle glades where, it seemed, no animal fiercer than flying foxes, monkeys or squirrels lived. The old woman had brought a serpent carved stick and pointed to the cobra's head which formed the handle and then to the thickets, shaking her head, grinning and mumbling. But did this negative gesture mean they were not to venture there, or that there were no serpents to fear? In any case, they were becoming fatalistic. It was impossible to restrain the children from exploring the island. They had soon discovered its well, a water-logged boat – impossible to use, Rosie decided regretfully – and a much larger, very elaborate state barge, similar to the one which had brought them to the island, but which was in a dilapidated state, lying grounded among the tangles of creepers along the western shore. However, the children enjoyed playing pirates and pretending to row with sticks of bamboo they dragged from the undergrowth.

Mrs Pettifer, the Chaplain's wife, had started morning classes for the older children. They did their sums on the marble floors, scrawling with bits of charcoal. They repeated their dates and their catechism, and some of them were able to recite as much of Tennyson's *Charge of the Light Brigade*, (then a very popular piece), as the ladies could jointly remember. But as the heat increased to what seemed boiling point, the children became hopelessly inattentive and it was easier to let them play in the dense green shade outside, where sometimes a cooling breeze blew in from the lake. The ladies' pooled supplies of soap were running low and they had soon used up their thread mending the children's clothes, torn by the thickets of their jungle playground. No one had dared to bathe since that unfortunate day when Rosie had been shepherding some of the children along the steps of the landing stage, paddling happily enough and some of them taking a dip, roped securely to Rosie and splashing merrily, when a wild shrieking sounded from the terrace above. Mrs Pettifer had scrambled down to haul her son Lionel ashore and turn angrily on Rosie. It seemed there were giant turtles in the lake – Mrs Pettifer had seen them with her own eyes – dangerous brutes with teeth like steel traps didn't Rosie know? Why, they could snap off a child's foot! Poor Captain Thompson had been swimming in a reservoir near Azampur not so long ago and one of them had – well, no matter, he would never be the same again . . . And now the moment her back was turned, here was Rosie letting Lionel run this appalling risk. Glaring at Rosie, she ordered the whole party indoors immediately.

During the fiercest noonday heat Rosie often left the rest of the women to their siesta, lying stifling among the glitter of the Rani's palace, to go out into the wilderness that had once been the formal parterres and waterways of an Indian garden. Lying on her burqa, she would watch the darting movements of the chipmunks, the tree frogs, and innumerable monkey families pursuing their activities in the leaves above, peering down at her, as she gazed up at them, with amused toleration. The flying foxes hung upside down sulkily, or wheeled and squabbled in the branches, swooping to suck the nectar from the flowers, slashing at a rival with their powerful thumb-hooks. At dusk they flapped down to drink in the lake, gliding over its surface, scooping up lappets of water. Once she had seen the surface suddenly heave. There was a flash and a snap and a flying fox vanished, leaving only a circle of ripples widening lazily. Rosie supposed it was one of the snapping turtles so dreaded by Mrs Pettifer and felt sick.

In general the animals of the island seemed kindly disposed towards the intruders. No terrifying insect pests had yet materialized, nor – strangely – were there any mosquitoes, however much Florence claimed the midges were such. None of the monkeys invaded the palace, contenting themselves with peeping through the grilles, and occasionally putting out a hesitant little paw to take the children's proffered titbits. (Watching to see that there was no foul play on either side, Rosie often remarked how clumsy the children's hands looked beside the delicately formed simian fingers, with their narrow filbert nails.)

But familiarity was not encouraged by the ladies, particularly after the loss of little Beatrice Mulligan-Jones's drawers. They'd been hung out with the rest of the wash and those wretched apes had whisked them off – it didn't matter so much about the bonnets and the handkerchiefs, but there really wasn't a shred of material left to make a new pair of drawers. It was particularly aggravating, too, to see the monkeys leaping about out of reach, studying their spoil intently, tearing at the lace, waving the garment around, or having a tug-of-war with the two legs till the seams finally gave way and only shreds of calico remained fluttering overhead like some banner, some victor's trophy – perhaps the banner of Hanuman, the monkey general now leading his forces against human prudishness. In any case, poor little Beatrice Mulligan-Jones was obliged to sit quietly indoors for some days until something could be contrived out of one of her several petticoats. She was only seven and sadly missed playing with the other children during this period of enforced inactivity. But then, there were standards to be maintained. It might be a deserted island, but neither Mrs Mulligan-Jones nor any other of the ladies even contemplated the idea of allowing their children to run wild.

Sometimes, wandering through the jungle paths, Rosie encountered the phantom pair grinding corn, or drawing water from the well. Like the island animals, they seemed indifferent to her presence and it was even more difficult to communicate with them. Once, pointing east to the mainland, where the Maharaja's palace lay golden in the evening sun, she tried to make them understand she wished to go there, but they appeared terrified and backed away into the jungle. That evening, overcome with a growing sense of helplessness and frustration – of exile from life itself – she did not join the ladies at supper. Miss Florence could sing for hers, thought Rosie, who resented more and more Florence's fragility, her habit of withdrawing into the corner she had marked as her own, lying there day in, day out, expecting Rosie to fan her, cosset her, and fetch her meals to her there. The children made so much noise, said Florence, closing her eyes wanly. When the others urged her to get up, to join them, to make an effort, she would shake her head, 'Just one of my bad days,' she would say, until at last they gave up trying to draw her out of herself. She might be a Viscount's daughter, but she was not setting a good example.

So Florence lay, languid and alone, in the alcove she had made her world. She never ventured outside. Everything alarmed her: insects, animals, vegetation – India. She was overwhelmed by its animal force. The sun burned into her flesh, beat at her brains and seeped away her willpower. The noise the smallest insect made was nerve racking in its intensity. The silence, the equally intense silence of some of the other creatures, however harmless they proved to be, was as frightening. Through the broken lattices she was aware of eyes, hundreds of small bright eyes always watching her, invading her thoughts, imposing themselves as surely in their silence as the more impudent monkeys who sometimes swung down to peer at her. The birds, too, flashed overhead, warbling, shrieking, cooing – a hundred different bird notes, but all invading her brain so that she could no longer hear the sounds of her own thoughts – the sounds of home: the soft muffled breathing of the cows in the meadow, the bell for morning prayers, a blackbird's song, the sound of carriage wheels on the gravel drive . . . home.

Now, peacock, nightingale, night jar, rock pigeon or fever bird – all hammered out the same overpowering alien note: India. Even the vegetation had a possessive force, creeping nearer each day, a surging, insatiable green tide, coiling round, invading the palace. Soon it would take possession entirely, overcoming the man-made marbles and even Florence herself. She shuddered. Great ropes of creeper and fleshy, cup-like blooms had spread across the windowsill and were flinging their tentacles round the lattice in a strangulating grip: green feelers, reaching in, reaching for her . . .

Over all lay the heat, the inescapable heat. That also took possession, so that Florence felt her body to be imprisoned in a clogging envelope of discomfort. Sweat trickled off her eyelids and blinded her, running down her spine clammily. The heat crept inwards too, pounding at her heart and turning her stomach. She had no stamina or willpower left. Soon she abandoned herself to it entirely and lay there scarcely caring. She no longer wept, she no longer had fever, or any of her 'little turns' or 'bad days'. All days were bad for her now. Florence was the living sacrifice that so many Hindu gods claimed.

But since Rosie was not the stuff of martyrs and preferred her own society to that of the ladies anyhow, she spent most of her time alone, wandering along the overgrown jungle paths, leaving her mistress to fend for herself. One evening she discovered a little promontory jutting out into the lake. At its tip, some princely whim had conceived a small octagonal gazebo overhanging the water. Its domed roof was ornamented with huge cut-crystal globes which sparkled in the last slanting grays of the sun. She pushed open the creaking door and the bats, finding their privacy invaded, flapped and squeaked about her head in helpless agitation.

Through the arched windows, Rosie watched the drama of an eastern twilight. The sky burned an incandescent lemon, then green, and at last fell to a luminous mauve, fading through this spectrum range in imperceptible but rapid stages. The parakeets came winging in on their homeward flight, flashing emerald as they circled among the scarlet coral trees. Rosie watched them longingly. They had flown over the town, over the rooftops of the Maharaja's palace and across its wide courtyards. Perhaps, in their flight, they had circled above the Rao Jagnabad standing there in all his pride. Where was he? Why did he not come here? How could she reach him? For the first time Rosie began to feel downcast. She had to admit that neither the strength of her desires nor the magic powers of the ring were strong enough to overcome the difficulties of her situation. Before, there had always been people to use, men on whom she could play, and some positive means of obtaining her ends. Now there was nothing. Nobody, no way, no way at all of escaping this beautiful prison – for such it had become, even to Rosie, who had loved its beauty and exoticism on sight. She had only to reach out, and pineapples, custard apples and mangoes fell into her hands; their strong, sweet smell was wafted to her now, overcoming the fragrance of the jasmine and moghra flowers, or the lime-scented shisham tree. It was indeed Paradise: but where was man?

Or rather, where was the Nine Tiger Man? Rosie leaned on the marble sill and looked across to the faraway horizons which were her prison bars. Westward, the afterglow was fading behind the hills. What lay beyond them? What cities were now up in arms, revenging themselves on the Europeans? What lay to the north? More cities, more bloodshed . . . and between them, how many miles of jungle, tiger country, where death waited, bamboo thickets where snakes struck and leopards prowled? She remembered how, on their flight from Delhi, they had camped on a hillside one night and heard a soft little cough nearby. The Sikhs had been on the alert at once. 'A leopard,' said Mr Edward, whispering so as not to wake Florence. The odd, deprecating little cough had sounded more like a pet cat with chest trouble, thought Rosie, but the Sikhs had said the leopard was one of the most ravening, dangerous foes.

She looked back, eastward, to where the lights of the town shone faintly. What lay there and beyond, were she ever to reach them? And what if the Rao was no longer there? All the strength of her passion had revived when she had caught sight of him, standing under the lantern as they embarked for the Rani's island. If only she could get hold of a boat – that little boat she had seen once on the shore of the bird islet! She felt certain the Rao had not recognized her, otherwise he must have been here before now. If ever she wanted to find him again, she would have to cross the lake herself. She had loved the tropic world of this island, but both the Rao and Shäitanpura had revealed another tropic world, a dimension of sensuality her ardent nature understood and craved. Rao or no, she must escape. Was she to spend the rest of her days rotting here? Mutineers, wild beasts, fevers – anything rather than this stagnation. She resolved that in the morning she would see what could be done about rigging up some sort of a raft, pieces of wood lashed together, perhaps, and a paddle made from smaller pieces fixed to a bamboo cane. Yes, she would manage something. Fortunately the lake was always smooth; no currents or storms ever ruffled its surface. As for Mrs Pettifer's man-eating turtles, well, she didn't suppose they'd snap at a raft.

She leaned out farther, watching the reflection of the evening star as it swayed and glittered on the surface of the lake. Beside it, the shadowy image of the kiosk was also reflected, starlight sparkling on the cut-crystal globes. As she watched, the reflections were shivered across by a stealthy movement beneath the surface. She peered down and saw, immediately below her, the largest and most unmistakable crocodile emerge from the water. This was certainly not one of Mrs Pettifer's turtles. It heaved its hideous glistening bulk up on to the shore, its scaly tail thrashing as its stumpy, claw-finished limbs propelled it along with a slithering rustle. Rosie had never seen a crocodile before, although there had been a very fair representation f one in a picture book at the orphanage; it had been part of a procession of docile beasts entering the Ark. This one did not look at all docile. As she stood there, her flesh creeping chill with terror, the beast became aware of her. It turned its head very slightly, and she caught the glint of one eye regarding her sideways. It remained very still, while Rosie wondered chokingly if it could climb. But with a rapid movement, at once violent and furtive, the great body slid back into the water and disappeared. As suddenly and with certitude, Rosie knew that the boat she had seen lying on the bird islet that first morning, the boat that had disappeared so strangely, had been no boat but one of these monsters. There could be no more thought of reaching the mainland on a homemade raft. She fled back to the palace, sobbing as she ran.

VII

Late one afternoon they heard the sound of music – flute, fiddle and drum. Faint, but unmistakable, it was carried across the water. It was coming from the mainland and it was coming nearer. The ladies rushed down to the landing stage, tripping over their petticoats in agitation. A boat was approaching: one of the Maharaja's state barges, similar to the one which had brought them to the Rani's island. Its red-and-gold prow was adorned with a gigantic carved tiger, leaping forward ferociously, cleaving the water. As the rowers pulled closer, turbaned figures could be seen grouped under an embroidered awning. Surely that must be the Maharaja himself, seated on a high-backed throne in the middle? So at last their long, lonely wait was over! He was arriving in person to bring them news of their husbands, of the rebellion and perhaps even to fetch them home.

Rosie was straining her eyes to distinguish the Rao Jagnabad's tall form among the group round the throne, but with their turbans and brocades and dark beards these Rajput men all looked the same from a distance. It never entered her head that he would not be there among the courtiers. Instinctively, she reached for the marriage-ring. For some time she had worn it hanging round her neck, tied on a strand of silk she had unravelled from the tassel of a cushion. She had almost begun to doubt its talismanic powers, but now she tugged it out of her bosom and began focusing the little mirror on the incoming boat.

'Now bring him here!' she wished and laughed triumphantly, certain that at last her wish was fulfilled.

Florence had not joined the general rush to the landing stage, but she had followed slowly, dreading what she might see.

She too believed that one day the Rao Jagnabad would materialize, a Satanic force, come to drive away that lethargy in which she had found a kind of peace. She stood on top of the steps, withdrawn, as always, from the rest, a spectator, an unwilling spectator even, of all life around her. Those large blue eyes which wept so easily were now fixed on the incoming boat almost reproachfully. What news would it bring? Was the Mutiny suppressed – and if so, at what price? Was Edward alive, or dead – or sending for her to join him in some other terrible place? Could she hope to go home? Could she possibly avoid seeing the Rao again?

The carved tiger sped nearer through the water and the children shrieked joyously as the boat came alongside below the line of trumpeting elephants. The musicians were playing furiously now, a sort of martial air, flute and drum predominating. The boatman made fast the barge and flung a silk-embroidered carpet across on to the landing stage, so that the nobles should disembark worthily. The group under the awning stood back and the seated figure rose, advanced to the side of the boat and with a sudden spring – the spring of a wild animal – cleared the barge and the carpet, and landed halfway up the steps in a flash of jewels and a clatter of weapons.

'Greetings, O memsahibs!' said the Rao Jagnabad. 'I come among you with joy in my heart. Bringing you messages from my adopted father the Prince of Princes – Raï-Raïan – the most noble Maharaja. I stay here among you for a time.'

The dramatic effect of this entry was not wasted on the ladies, who had fallen back in alarm at his jack-in-the-box spring, but were immediately reassured by his polite address and splendid appearance. This was indeed magnificent. Rosie, gazing at her lover standing there lit by the strong evening sun, glittering with jewels, vibrant with life, felt giddy at the prospect before her. Yes, she'd always known it, from the moment she'd clapped eyes on him through the conservatory window; she'd always known they would come together for good, or ill. The

Rao made no sign that he had seen her, nor did he appear to notice Florence, pressed back against the huge leaves of a banana tree at the top of the steps. But Rosie was not worried. There was plenty of time. The ladies crowded round the Rao Jagnabad, making polite conversation and leading him towards the palace, while his suite, the nobles and the royal guards, followed at a respectful distance, the children hopping round. At the entrance to the palace, the aged phantoms were discovered flat on their faces, prostrated on the marble threshold. Much to the ladies' surprise, the Rao neither raised them nor stepped over them. Instead, he deliberately trod on their crumpled forms with a strange movement, as if trampling them underfoot. Seeing the ladies' astonished faces, he said, 'They do homage and I receive it. It is the manner of their country. They come from a long way country in Tibet. They were slaves of deceased Rani.' He proceeded into the mirrored hall. Kicking the bolsters and cushions into a mound at one end of the room, he seated himself upon them in a curious upright yet crouched attitude, as if still ready to spring. He unbuckled his diamond-hilted sword and laid it beside him, but they noticed his hand still caressed it lovingly. Such was his air of majesty that he had now transformed the pile of cushions into a throne and the mirrored room into a hall of audience. When two of his suite hurried forward to support the golden umbrella of state over his head, the illusion was complete. The slanted, seemingly sleepy yet baleful stare of the tiger ranged round the room and over the assembly. Abruptly, the savage mask gave place to a charming smile. He clapped his hands.

'I am hungry, we eat!' he announced. The Tibetans scuttled out to do his bidding, while the guards brought in a number of large baskets with many kinds of dishes prepared in the Maharaja's kitchens. Some were tied up in muslin handkerchiefs, scarlet and yellow and violet, spangled in gold, while others were folded in large glossy leaves. While the ladies and children stared avidly at this succulent spectacle, the

Rajput nobles were staring around with equal avidity. They had never set foot on the Rani's island, much less in her palace, or indeed in any zenana but their own. Besides, they found the presence of so many memsahibs most intriguing.

The Rao's glance roved over the ladies with a proprietary air, but still he did not single out either Florence or Rosie. Nor did he seem in any hurry to deliver the promised messages. No one ventured to broach the question of the Mutiny, for he was a rather intimidating figure who, they felt, must on no account be provoked. The ladies decided on tact. Besides, most of them had learned from married life that gentlemen are seldom approachable until fed. It would be wiser to wait till the Rao had eaten.

The guards now spread out a splendid feast, lit by coloured glass lanterns placed among the dishes on the floor. The fiddlers scraped away at their one-stringed sarangis, the drummers' brown fingers rattled back and forth over the drums and the flutists – dusky Papagenos – sounded their sweet and haunting notes. The nobles sat cross-legged among the women, offering them delicacies – sohan halva and papadums stuffed with saffron and cinnamon. To drink, there was the traditional liquor of the Indian princes – aska – composed of the essence of centuries-old pressed fruits, chickens, and powdered precious stones; a drink as rare as it was strange. The ladies sipped apprehensively from little jade, jewel-studded cups and felt dashing. Soon they were sufficiently mellowed to agree that their children should share in the treats. The Rajput warriors were now offering indigestible titbits to the children and smiling their strangely childish, innocent smiles, so that they seemed to be like so many children themselves; bearded ones, perhaps, but certainly not the redoubtable warriors they were in fact. Florence had placed herself well back, out of the lantern light and hidden, she hoped, by Mrs Pettifer's ample form. When the musicians paused to drink sherbet, she thought the whole hall must hear her heart thudding. She could certainly hear the creak of Mrs Pettifer's stays.

Now fed, the Rao began to speak. The Maharaja was convened to a meeting of British army chiefs, a week's journey to the north. He had taken most of his troops with him, and was raising men on the way. He was likely to be gone some time. Meanwhile, he had entrusted his kingdom to the Rao, his adopted son and heir, and he had charged him to visit the memsahibs and enquire if they lacked anything. He brought them no news of their husbands, but told them the fighting was widespread and terrible. Far from being over, the Mutiny was gathering force. Delhi was still in the hands of the rebels. The British were camped on the Ridge and no one knew why they did not attack. Many regiments had been disbanded, even disarmed. 'A sadness mistake,' said the Rao, explaining that many who, like his Rajput troops, were loyal, had now been falsely accused, hanged, or blown from the mouth of a cannon. Others had dispersed to their villages in bitterness and were turning against the British. Lucknow was besieged and still held out. General Havelock had arrived at Cawnpore too late to stop the massacre, but was believed to be marching to relieve Lucknow. Nicholson – the great Nikalseyn, whom the Sikhs worshipped as a god – was said to be riding down from the Punjab to avenge Delhi . . . The Rao paused dramatically, 'And when he does,' he continued, 'then all India will be at peace, and you shall lie again with your husbands, O memsahibs.'

The ladies thought it an unfortunate turn of phrase, but they appreciated his sincerity. Such a handsome creature! What eyes! What a muscular form! It seemed a long time since they had seen a man, a much longer time since any man had looked at them as this one did. Instinctively they began to preen.

'In meantime,' he continued 'you want for no thing I believe?' And the ladies felt they could not explain to so godlike a figure that they needed a hundred insignificant objects such as stay-laces, hairpins, headache powders, soap and materials for new clothes all round.

However, the Rao had not been described, (by certain

suspicious British husbands), as 'a ladies' man' for nothing. He had forestalled some of their wishes most lavishly. The guards now brought in a number of round woven baskets which revealed a resplendent collection of saris. Some were of finest muslin, gauzy and splashed with silver thread; some of kincob, like molten metal, being entirely woven with gold; some were patterned with flowers, pink roses audaciously scattered on a scarlet ground; others were bordered with fringes of seed pearls. There were round peacock feather fans; heavy, clashing ankle bracelets and great ropes of rough-cut precious stones, bracelets and ear rings; nose rings, too, thought the ladies, eyeing these trappings of a princely zenana spread out before them.

The Rao began to distribute his gifts with ceremony. Bowing, salaaming, fixing each woman with his dark possessive glance, he called them to him one by one, holding up this sari, or that jewel, against them, until he thought his choice became them. The ladies blushed with pleasure, although they thought the presents far too handsome and really, not much use to them on the island. Also, they did not think their husbands would care for them to accept jewellery. Still, it was most thoughtful, most generous.

The children, too, had not been forgotten. There were baskets full of toys, the gaily painted papier-mâché toys of the Indian bazaars, striped tigers and spotted pards; little brass horses on wheels, kites, and tin trumpets and drums for the boys, which now kept them happy, if not quiet. There were also some very unsuitable little human figures, evidently something to do with the great festival of Holi and all those fertility cults. Really! What an idea, giving them as toys! The ladies managed to remove them when the children were not looking. The *pièce de résistance* was a wooden elephant about the size of a large St Bernard dog. It was set on rockers in the manner of a rocking horse, its jewelled ornaments painted with loving care, as were its gilded nails and pink-lined trunk. Its large stiff ears stood away from its head like tropical leaves and its tiny eyes were as roguish and kind as those of a real elephant. It was infinitely pleasing and the children crowded round, fighting to climb on 'Jumbo's' back.

In the midst of this pandemonium Florence faced the dreaded moment of recognition. She was obliged to come forward in her turn. Standing before the Nine Tiger Man, receive from his hand a blue and gold sari.

'So! It is Miss Florence Memsahib,' he said, joining his hands together in the beautiful Indian gesture of greeting. Yet his inscrutable face showed no surprise to find her there.

'I am happy, I repay the hospitality of your most-honoured mother's house,' he said, holding another coloured sari against her face, which was now deadly pale. He shook his head, flung aside a yellow sari, substituting for it one of a pale lilac colour. Then, placing a swag of twisted pearls round her neck, he bowed and led her ceremoniously to a cushioned alcove where he ordered one of his suite to fan her.

The ladies were twittering with ill-concealed curiosity. So little Mrs Mulgrove knew him all along! And he'd been at her mother's house in England! Well, no doubt he would look after them all with special care, now. They regretted not having made more efforts to draw Florence into their circle and quite forgave her those standoffish airs.

All this time Rosie had been standing aside, unremarked, it seemed. In view of her being what the ladies thought of as 'a lower-class girl', it was quite proper that she should be the last to receive a gift – if indeed she was to receive one at all. But when the Rao motioned her forward they could scarcely believe their eyes.

'Rosee! The same Rosee!' he said, smiling. To the ladies' amazement they saw Rosie laughing back, bold and sly, as if somehow they shared a secret. The hussy! But there was worse to come. The Rao threw a particularly sumptuous pink and gold sari across her shoulders and followed this by a cascade of emeralds, dripping pearls.

'Rani again,' he said mysteriously. Rosie nodded, laughing up at him, bold as brass. Moreover, she said something they could not follow – something in that Hindustani she'd picked up somehow or other. Showing off, as usual, thought the ladies. The Rao looked astonished and then pleased. He spoke to her in his own tongue and she seemed able to reply. The assembled courtiers followed this exchange with delighted interest, while the ladies were more mystified than ever.

By now the Rao Jagnabad was plainly in a high good humour. He called for his hookah and ordered the musicians to play. Some of the nobles began to sing the long, slow, unwinding *mélopées* of the East which the Rao applauded vigorously; puffing at his hookah and listening with the half-closed eyes of a tiger sunning itself. Turning to the ladies and bowing, he suggested they too should sing – something from their own country, a song of home? It was in fact an order, but this they did not understand, and hung back coyly, overcome with confusion, at which he glowered.

Shyness, however, was not something from which Rosie suffered. Before the atmosphere could become too tense, she had jumped to her feet and, addressing herself to the Rao, all smiles and *most* impertinently, as the ladies said later, she launched into a popular song the servants' hall had much enjoyed hearing Henry render when he returned from a visit to a London music hall.

'The boy I love is up in the gallery,' sang Rosie, waving and nodding to the princely figure seated on the pile of cushions.

'The boy I love is up in the gallery,
The boy I love is smiling down at me.
There he is, plain to see,
A-waving of his handkerchee–'

She got no further with this artless ditty, for with a roar of applause and shouts of 'Wah! Wah! Shabash!' from the courtiers, who were equally entranced, the Rao Jagnabad sprang forward, lifted Rosie high above his head and then flung her down on the cushions beside him.

Such behaviour both startled and horrified the ladies, but before they could decide what line of disciplinary action should be taken with Rosie, Florence was seen to have fainted.

When she came round the news which greeted her was enough to make her faint once more. It seemed that the Rao had dismissed his suite, courtiers, musicians and guests, and sent them all back to the mainland.

'I am well here,' he had said. 'I shall stay for many moons. And,' he added looking round at their astonished faces, 'I am seeing many memsahibs to care for me.'

At which, said the ladies, now busy restoring Florence by waving burnt peacock feathers under her nose at which, (imagine such a thing!), he had seized hold of Rosie in a most lascivious manner and begun kissing her, in front of the children too! No one knew where to look . . . And now the boat had gone and they were left alone with this monster of depravity. Fortunately, he was upstairs at this moment. With Rosie. They could be heard, distinctly, carrying on in the most shameless manner.

All that night the ladies lay fuming amid their finery. They had decided, as one, to give back the presents. At breakfast time moral indignation knew no bounds when Rosie appeared, her hair hanging down, wrapped far too loosely in the pink sari, beneath which it was plain to see she wore nothing.

'Breakfast!' she said gaily, 'His Highness is hungry and so am I.' She began turning over the baskets and leafy platters of last night's feast, and having loaded a tray with the best of what was left, without so much as by-your-leave, she returned upstairs, her mouth full of sugared cinnamon curd cakes. It was insupportable.

But alas! The ladies were now obliged to support this and a lot more almost too horrible to relate. The Rao, it was soon evident, intended to enjoy his unique position on the island. This was to be his zenana and they were to be its members – 'curtain wives', as they were traditionally known in India. Rosie was to reign as Rani. Or chief concubine, as Mrs Tollemache, the Colonel's wife, said with bitterness. Before, in matters of authority, she had always taken the lead, for the military protocol of Azampur had been preserved. Mrs Pettifer, being the Chaplain's wife, had come second thus, it was felt, upholding both temporal and spiritual power. Florence, if she had not been so retiring, could have taken the social lead . . . But now?

As King of the Castle, the Nine Tiger Man set about arranging matters to his satisfaction. When the Tibetans had produced a bunch of huge rusted keys, he had stalked about the place opening long-shut doors and revealing unsuspected rooms. Below the looking glass hall, the Hall of the Peacocks as he called it, which was the memsahibs' quarters, a whole subterranean world of dark passages was now disclosed. Prison vaults, cellars for preserving ice and a curious room fitted up with bellows and a tank set below a grilled ceiling. This was immediately beneath the Rani's dressing room and here, in the past, her slaves had, by means of the bellows, puffed perfumed air from a tankful of precious essence, up through the grille to where the Rani's silks were suspended above, absorbing the attar of roses, sandalwood, or musk – so essential to Indian coquetry and elegance. Great sealed vats of perfumes were still stored round the walls. Soon Mrs Pettifer, or any other of the less agreeable memsahibs, (the Rao took Rosie's advice in this matter), were to be seen labouring away at the bellows while Rosie's saris now hanging in the Rani's dressing room were impregnated with fragrance.

The largest of the subterranean rooms was the taikhana: a long cool hall such as was traditionally found in old Indian houses, designed as a retreat from the fiercest heat. Here the children were banished with their toys, the Rao unbending so far as to install the elephant rocking horse himself, for it was made of teak and so heavy that the combined efforts of the ladies and the aged phantoms could not get it down the stairs. In spite of their resentment at the children's banishment, the ladies were thankful, for it kept them away from the scenes – the debauches – which now took place upstairs. On the terrace, the silver swing had been polished and set to rights, to become the focal point of whole days and nights of voluptuous dalliance; for, said the Rao, it was now the month of Sawan, of the Tij, or Swing Festival. But the ladies had by now lost all count of time.

It was presently seen that the Rao exercised a positively mesmeric effect over his zenana, for not one of them could dispute his will – not even Mrs Tollemache, until then sustained by a particularly vigorous will of her own. They were his slaves, as well as his concubines. Oh, the horror of it all . . . the unimaginable shame! Yet what else could they do, but submit? There were the children to think of and then, he wore a dagger at his waist, which he sometimes brandished in a most threatening manner. Still, they could scarcely believe their eyes when they saw Florence, (a viscount's daughter, too!), standing meekly in the alcove where he sprawled with Rosie – her own maid – fanning them, wielding the long sheaf of peacock feathers bound in gold which were the prerogative of kings.

The Rao was insistent on all the attributes of rank. When he walked abroad in the early morning sunlight, one of the ladies must always follow a pace behind, holding the golden umbrella of Majesty over his head. In the Maharaja's absence from his kingdom, the Rao was his viceroy, symbol of his might. The ladies must address him as 'Presence', 'Prince of Princes', 'Sun of Majesty', or some equally fulsome phrase, which enraged them. Moreover, they must make obeisance before him, laying their heads on his foot, speak only when addressed by him, eat only after he and Rosie had been served, show deference to Rosie as the first favourite, obey the Rao's every wish . . . in short, conduct themselves as was expected of the lowly and submissive members of his zenana they had become.

There were certain things which rankled deeply. The nautch, for instance. The Rao had seemed to take a particular pleasure in tormenting them, making them dance for him ('like so many bayadères,' as the Chaplain's wife remarked bitterly). They were aware they looked ridiculous, twirling and posturing self consciously, the heavy bracelets tinkling on their ankles which, however trim, appeared clumsy compared to the delicate, bird-boned limbs of Indian women. While the Tibetans, who had been pressed into service as musicians, beat monotonously on a gourd drum, or rattled a tambourine, the ladies tried desperately to invent steps which suited these outlandish rhythms. Nothing they had ever known before, no polka, waltz, jig, schottische – not even a Highland fling – seemed to fit. It was very discouraging. Worst of all, even worse than performing under the Rao's impassive gaze, was the fact that Rosie was watching too, her green eyes mischievous, lolling back beside her lover, sharing a dish of fruit with him and sometimes feeding him especially luscious mouthfuls, licking her fingers or wiping them on the cushions in the most vulgar manner. The ladies all agreed: it was disgusting – it was too degrading – that she should queen it over them. They would almost rather submit to those awful caresses than have to put up with this. The other – the other thing – well, that was different. They did not feel ridiculous then. They saw themselves as victims of a satyr's lust; tragic figures, trapped, helpless, betrayed – but not ridiculous.

They had been ordered to don their saris and jewels as every day wear. 'To make beautiful,' in the Rao's words. Although some of them clung most obstinately to their corsets and drawers, most of them soon found it was almost impossible to wear a sari over such bulky underwear; and much cooler without, anyhow. Rosie, with her habitual good nature, now offered to show them how to drape the seven-yard silks, for there were a number of ways, but they could scarcely bear her to come near them.

'Strumpet! Slut! *Whore!* Don't you dare touch me!' shouted Mrs Tollemache, quite beside herself with virtuous indignation and having exhausted her vocabulary of abuse, sank back clutching at her heart. These dreadful words – words which none of the other ladies had ever pronounced themselves – were, it was generally felt, deserved. But Rosie seemed quite unrepentant, merely contenting herself with jabbing a pin into Mrs Tollemache in passing, as she set about draping the more compliant ladies. And what if I am? she thought lazily. She was entirely happy in this strange situation, with no thought for yesterday or tomorrow, returning, with the Rao to that limboland of the senses they had shared together, so briefly, in the blue-curtained room at Bogwood; and which she had sought to recapture in Shäitanpura.

At evening they would go out on to the rooftop and, like generations of India's lovers before them, lie together among the cushions, under a rising moon. Or, entwined in the silver swing, sway languidly back and forth among the fireflies, listening to the thousand small sounds of the jungle below. Sometimes the Rao would tire abruptly of this idyll and clap his hands, at which one of the ladies stationed below would have to climb the stairs and execute his commands. There was no telling what these might be. Perhaps to strew the terrace with rose leaves, to fetch sherbet, push the swing, or sing. The ladies' repertoire was limited and generally unsuited to the occasion.

Although no doubt ballads such as 'The Lass of Richmond Hill' or 'Green Grow the Rushes O!' sounded equally exotic to the Rao's untutored ear.

But sometimes the ladies were not let off so easily. These were the most searing occasions when the Rao ordered them to join Rosie and himself in their revels. The ladies were beyond speech . . . but the Rao had very much enjoyed it all. He had particularly enjoyed rousing Rosie's jealousy, for the monogamous instincts of the West were something quite new to him. He had heard that European ladies did not care to share and so it seemed for, at first, Rosie had been inclined to sulk. But after a very short while she only laughed. She soon realized she need fear no rivals among them. Besides, she relished being able to repay their snubbings in this most unexpected manner. And what a fuss the ladies made! For ever snivelling, thought Rosie. Married ladies, too – they can't pretend they don't know what it's all about. And then, remembering the Reverend Augustus Pettifer, Colonel Marmaduke Tollemache, Major Potts and most of the other husbands she had seen at Azampur, she decided that after all, perhaps their wives really had no idea, no kind of notion. 'Well anyhow, it will be a nice surprise,' she remarked to the Rao. And they laughed together, the unconstrained merry laughter of savages.

Still, sometimes Rosie couldn't help feeling sorry for Miss Florence. My word, she did look queer these days, just as if she'd seen a ghost! And perhaps she had the ghost of her girlish imaginings. She crept about, never raising her eyes, never speaking, even to Rosie. Yet it was obvious that the Rao accorded her a certain respect which he allowed none of the others. If Rosie was his favourite concubine, then Florence was a particularly favoured slave. True, many of the most menial tasks were hers, sweeping the paths, or polishing the silver swing, and she was sent fetching and carrying at all hours. But although the Rao seldom spoke to her, he had appointed her to the charge of his hookah, an office she fulfilled with unexpected skill. She alone, it seemed, could mix the blend of tobacco and aromatic spices he liked, or knew the precise proportion of rosewater to cool the pipe. The complicated coils of this water pipe, the neytchah, with its mounh-nal, or amber mouthpiece, and the tehilem where the embers glowed, had seemed baffling even to Rosie, with her eastern initiation in Shäitanpura. Yet now she saw to her astonishment that Florence performed this specialized ritual as naturally as if she had been presiding over her own tea table. The Rao marked his approbation by naming her his Hookah-berdar, the slave who generally accompanies the master everywhere he goes, in a palanquin, on horseback, visiting, or hunting – but is always there, holding the hookah in readiness. Since the Nine Tiger Man never quitted the island, nor hunted and seldom stirred from the terrace rooftop, Florence was generally to be seen sitting huddled at the foot of the stairs, awaiting his orders, which sounded oddly, when he shouted, not without irony, 'Hey, Memsahib Hookah-berdar!' and Florence would rush up the stairs, obedient to his command. As always, she held herself aloof from all the rest of the ladies. Although she now sometimes witnessed some very strange scenes, she had not yet been required to participate.

'Why not?' Rosie asked the Rao Jagnabad one sultry siesta hour as they lay in a lacquered bed, sole piece of furniture in the small turret room which had been the Rani's bedroom. Now the Rao had chosen it for his own. It was set a little apart from the rest of the palace and beyond the deeply embrasured windows, the western shores of the lake, the mountains and the sunset were disclosed in all their loveliness. The walls were frescoed with scenes of Indian life: life-size dancing girls in provoking poses flanked the bed; jungles and waterfalls crowded round, with tiger families sporting in the greenery, or being slain by princes on elephant back; troops were engaged in mortal combat; and lovers caressed each other with equal fury on rooftops resembling that one where Rosie and the Rao so often lay locked in love.

'Why not? Why don't you fancy Miss Florence?' Rosie persisted.

The Rao frowned. 'She loves too strong,' was his odd reply.

'But how do you know?' Rosie was becoming uneasy, wondering if, after all, he had found the letter.

He smiled down at her. Yet there was something implacable in the smile – the hunter's smile. 'I am more happy with you, Rosee. The others, too, they are pleasing me.'

'But surely you don't want all of them?' asked Rosie, who was beginning to doubt, not so much her lover's prowess, as his taste.

'All – all! Every memsahib,' replied the Rao, looking particularly wild.

Rosie had discovered that he had felt slighted in England, that now he was revenging himself. Patronage: she knew what that was. Not only the gentry, but the hierarchy of the servants' hall had patronized her long enough. It was only on reaching India – and in Shäitanpura particularly, that she had felt freed from patronage. But at Azampur it had begun all over again with the ladies.

It seemed that all the official interest accorded the Rao Jagnabad in England, the receptions, the hospitality, the inviting glances of so many high-born ladies – even honorary membership of the Travellers' Club – had not lessened his sense of slight. To them, he knew, he was a native, to be patronized amiably, but never, never to be regarded as an equal. His dark skin, 'the burnished livery of the sun', as the Dowager had reminded him in Shakespeare's graceful phrase, was responsible for the wounding way he had been suddenly dropped by several ladies who had certainly led him to hope . . . . In any case, he bore a grudge. His country was good enough for Englishmen to covet and to possess, as were the women of his country. But he must not covet, much less possess, the memsahibs. Until now. Now, the ladies were thoroughly tamed. It was not, he said, so much a question of taste as of principle.

Certainly he had not found all the ladies from Azampur to his liking, but vengeance was sweet. He was systematically revenging himself and his race for many years of humiliation. He did not choose to make them grind corn, one of the Mutineers' favourite methods of abasing the memsahibs. He had surer ways.

In a sense, it was the Rao's own Mutiny.

'And afterwards,' he said, lingering voluptuously over the thought, 'when they tell their husbands what I am doing, I am revenged!'

'I shouldn't be so sure they'll tell,' said Rosie.

The Rao's face fell. It would be terrible if he'd taken all that trouble for nothing. Terrible . . .

'But I thought memsahibs were so truthful ladies,' he said, looking pathetically distressed.

'Well, it's all according,' replied Rosie soothingly. She was gazing up at the painted ceiling, only half listening to all this talk of revenge. Placed above the bed was a star-shaped mirror circled in painted wreaths of flowers and birds. It reflected the Rao's dark body beside her own. How he did run on. It was sinful to waste words at a time like this.

While the Rao Jagnabad ruled as absolute monarch in this kingdom of the senses, the ladies of his unusual zenana alternated between fits of despair, anxiety, elation and acute loneliness. For the presence of one man, although a demanding one, could scarcely be described as company in their sense of the word. Besides, they had to share him. The rains were not far off now and the heat gathered round them with a ferocity from which there was no escape. Still no boat called and still they were as cut off from the mainland as before the Rao's arrival. Although this was all for the best, they decided, for thus their mass downfall remained unperceived, except by the aged phantoms, who seemed as indifferent as usual when they shuffled in with the chupatties.

Although the Rao was clearly a man of strong appetites, another Heliogabalus, as Mrs Pritchett, the adjutant's wife, remarked, he ate the leathery chupatties and nameless messes of curry without comment and made no effort to improve the commissariat. But then, as they reminded each other, he was a native – he didn't know any better. Strangely enough, in view of the horrors of their situation, the ladies were looking remarkably well and seemed to have bloomed in misfortune. Still, they felt the need for better, more sustaining food. None of them ventured to suggest to the Rao that they might take on the cooking; and in any case supplies were of the most limited nature. Among themselves they spoke longingly of nourishing chicken broths, a nice roast, jellies . . . but although the oranges lay rotting beneath the lacquered leaves, they were no nearer achieving so much as marmalade for their breakfast. Even pigeon pie was denied them. The Rao protected the birds most strictly. 'For they were our postmen in long ago,' he said. Quoting the Emperor Akbar, he added, 'Why should we be sepulchres for beasts and birds?' So the ladies languished on a strictly vegetarian diet and sometimes felt quite faint.

Keeping the true situation from the children was another problem, but in spite of a growing yet unavowed rivalry among themselves, the ladies were as one on this point. They took it in turns to watch over the children who played unconcerned in the taikhana, or were hurried off for an airing on the farther point of the island, away from the contaminating atmosphere of the palace.

'Mama musn't be disturbed just now, Mama is busy,' was the agreed formula when any of the children happened to ask for a parent who was occupied elsewhere at the Rao's command. The children did not seem aware of anything unusual and soon became accustomed to seeing their mothers in saris – and little else. They themselves were still rigorously buttoned into their European garments; although watching them struggle through the tropic vegetation in boots, petticoats, long pants and straw hats, the Rao had suggested they might be better off in loincloths. The very idea! said their mothers. They might be fallen women, but no one should ever say they neglected their children. So they buttoned them up tight and sent them out to risk prickly heat and sunstroke.

They resented the Rao Jagnabad's popularity among their children. They rightly thought him a dangerous influence and disapproved when the children persisted in calling him 'Uncle'. In the few hours he could spare from more adult distractions he flew kites with them, showed them how to scale coconut palms, or told them deliciously alarming stories about a spirit, the Churel, who walked with its feet turned back to front; or the Nagas — serpents who live in a splendid underground realm, Patala, where the lords of the serpent world, Vasuki, Sankha, Kulika and Mahasanka, possess the finest precious stones in all the world. The children now assumed these names and played snake kingdoms, begging to be allowed to wear their mother's jewels and writhing and hissing most convincingly among themselves. Their mothers had to admit that deplorable as was his conduct towards themselves, the Rao knew how to keep the children happy.

VIII

After some weeks of life entirely on his own terms, the Rao Jagnabad began to feel himself sufficiently revenged on the English nation as a whole. The purely academic pleasure of humiliating the memsahibs had begun to pall. Perhaps, too, he was wearying of them because they showed signs of becoming less unwilling. After all the tears and protests, he noticed they were answering his summons with increasing alacrity, although they would never master the arts of pleasing: they lacked both the fire and the languorous docility inherent in the women of his own race, who were born and bred for the sole purpose of delighting man. Not that pleasure was the first object of his visit to the Rani's island either. Revenge – that took pride of place – but if, as he suspected, the memsahibs really were starting to quarrel among themselves for his favours, then the zest had gone from this revenge.

All the ladies had shared his favours now, except Florence. Something, he could not say what, kept him from sending for Florence. Perhaps it was because, in England, she had never patronized him, or led him on, either. Or was it that he was grateful for the way her mother, the Dowager, had supported him, pleading his cause in the highest places? In any case, he felt no desire to revenge himself by way of Florence. Then, too, he had sensed from the beginning, from the Bogwood house party, that in spite of her apparent insipidity, she could love passionately – violently – and that her heart was his. The tyranny, the octopus tentacles of such love, were something he fled instinctively.

The Rao had never been in love and the idea alarmed him. In his brief, triumphant rise to power as the Maharaja's heir he had divided women into two categories: those with bodies and those with jewels. And the women, in their turn, had wanted one or other of these two things from him. Except in London, he had always found this a perfectly satisfactory arrangement.

But suddenly, as if a curtain had been pulled aside, he perceived a strange and radiant horizon – a whole new world of perfect love. Could that be? It was something entirely different and all at once he desired it ardently. He wanted Florence's love: it would be interesting to see if her love overcame her scruples which he felt must be strong, judging by what he had seen of her background at Bogwood. Then, too, was this going to make Rosie jealous at last? The whole prospect enchanted him. Ruthlessly he shook her awake.

'Bring Memsahib Florence here quick,' he said. Hearing his tone, Rosie hastened to obey.

Whatever is he up to now, she thought, as she stumbled down the stairs. Up to no good, anyhow, she decided, and hoped Florence wouldn't be such a fool as to tell him about the letter. It wouldn't help matters and it might even cause trouble between herself and the Rao. Florence did not weep when Rosie led her up to the turret, but she trembled convulsively.

'It's all right, Miss Florence – you'll see, everything will be quite simple if you don't go making difficulties,' Rosie told her kindly, trying to be comforting.

One thing's for certain, he'll soon loose patience with that namby pamby, thought Rosie, when the Rao told her to leave them alone.

But it was just this quality of simplicity, of innocence which, like many voluptuaries before him, the Rao found so irresistible. He had never imagined any woman could be quite so innocent – so determined, too. Florence was like nothing he had ever encountered. She did not resist him, she simply removed herself. He held an empty shell in his arms, a pale opalescent shell. He wooed her with all the force of his growing infatuation and she simply seemed to look through him with those limpid blue eyes which, he now thought, were the exact colour of the lake. Poetry and passion grew in the Rao's awakening soul as he struggled to regain his former ruthlessness. To his dismay, he found himself treating her with more and more respect.

It was unthinkable! Whole days and nights now passed in this frustrating fashion, the Rao invoking his gods, beseeching them to restore to him that merciless, carefree cruelty which distinguishes the hunter; while Florence, lying in the lacquered bed, resembling a china doll and with about as much animation, waged her own war. Beneath the porcelain façade, Florence too was in turmoil and fighting a losing battle. While the Rao strove to overcome his newfound scruples, to become once again the Nine Tiger Man who lorded it over all women, Florence strove to conceal her true feelings, which were of the same tumultuous force as when they had first overtaken her at the Duchess of Sutherland's ball. But she had her pride.

She told herself over and over again that this was the man who had humiliated her so cruelly, ignoring her letter, the avowal of her love which it had cost her so dear to make. Now it was too late. She was a married woman. Besides, he had been behaving in the most shocking manner with the other ladies – and with Rosie in particular – her own maid, a servant-girl! This was quite unforgivable to Florence whose awareness of class distinctions was typically British and quite as strong, as clearly defined, as the caste-systems of India. He was uncivilized, a monster, a cruel and violent barbarian, the embodiment of the hated East, of dreadful India where she was so miserable. Besides, she simply must remember, she was Edward's wife . . . Only last year just before she left home there had been talk of introducing a bill in Parliament to enforce the death penalty for adultery. Many people had thought it an excellent idea . . . She wondered if the bill had been passed. Then how, precisely, define adultery? Clearly, the twenty-three ladies, her companions on the Rani's island, who had all been obliged to comply with the Rao's demands, were technically adulterous. While she, lying here, adored and adoring but still respected, was not. Yet if the strength of her desires were taken into account, she would be in the condemned cell by now. It was all very puzzling.

She really did not know what to think any more. Here she was, Florence Emily Ada Mulgrove who only last year, as a *jeune fille*, had been sent out of the room by Mama if the guests showed signs of discussing subjects of the least animation. Now, barely four months married to Edward, she was lying in a red-and-gold lacquered bed beside a Hindu prince – a monster of depravity – and still what the other ladies described (in detail) as the Worst had not occurred. What could it mean? What did the Rao want? He seemed positively timid at times, not at all the way he had been behaving with the others. Now he seemed content just to sit beside her, cradling her hand in both his own, carefully, as if it were some treasure. He would hold it up against the light, saying it was transparent, luminous like white jade, like alabaster. Or he would simply gaze at her by the hour; plait and unplait her long ash-blonde hair; or wind her in different coloured saris, and opening more and more coffers, festoon her with larger and even more barbaric jewels until she felt crushed. What with the weight of these adornments, the sultry, thunderous atmosphere and the force of both their pent-up emotions, Florence was completely worn out and lay there, looking waxen in her fragility. While finding her pallor the most romantic, the most lovely thing he had ever seen, the Rao hung over her anxiously, ordering Rose upstairs to fan her while he conferred with the Tibetans, concocting herbal mixtures which he hoped would prove restorative. And it must be said to his credit that he refused recourse to any of the love potions and aphrodisiacs with which, in the East, it was customary to inflame the unresponsive object of one's affection. No, if Florence Memsahib did not offer him her love, he would not ask for it, much less force her to him . . . Waving aside the pan leaves, the powdered rhinoceros horn and dried tiger's flesh which were all the Tibetans could provide for the moment, he dashed back to the palace on the wings of love. He could hardly bear to be away from Florence for an instant. Now it was he who was jealous, possessive, resenting even her maid's presence. Snatching the fan out of the bewildered Rosie's hand, he sent her packing and set to fanning his beloved himself.

There was a long-necked, graceful stringed instrument, a sita, hanging on the painted wall. Sometimes he played and sang – the plaintive half-tones of Indian love songs, Florence guessed them to be. He sang them softly, yearningly, so that she felt all her resolves crumbling, and she closed her eyes to shut out the vision of her suppliant. So this abortive romance continued, Florence wilting visibly, until the Rao began to fearsome malign god threatened them; that his pearl, his silver angel, would be snatched from him before he could win the love he so ardently desired but did not know how to obtain.

It was the stifling silent hour of mid afternoon, when the sky seemed to press lower over the earth and the birds were silent among the trees where no leaf stirred. Florence lay under an awning, waiting for the evening breeze. The Rao crouched beside her and smiled; that odd, appealing, almost innocent smile which sometimes replaced the tiger's mask. They were watching a small green lizard which was watching them. But however still a human being remains, it cannot achieve the absolute immobility of lizards. Even the imperceptible blink of an eyelid is perceived by such creatures, to whom the rise and fall of a breathing body probably appears magnified into some volcanic heave, while the eyelid's flicker becomes the rising and falling of a giant curtain. Florence threw it a piece of crumbled chupatty, but it did not move until, with a flash of colour, it was gone. Florence was learning to overcome her fear of the lizards and geckoes which appeared in large numbers to sun themselves and sometimes crawled over the glass lanterns, warming their little yellow bellies against the light. Scaled down, the lizards were like tiny crocodiles; crocodiles for dolls, said Florence. The infatuated Rao thought it the most adorable idea imaginable. Dolly crocodiles! He stroked her hand lovingly and she did not withdraw it.

'Florensse– ' he pronounced her name in a special way she loved, '– are you not in happiness with me, Florensse? I want that you are happy. I want that you love me strong like I am loving you, my Angel Florensse . . . My Indrani, my Queen of Paradise, I want that I make Paradise for you.'

Florence did not reply. She felt choked-choked with love. It was useless . . . the worst *had* happened. She could no longer fight. She simply must let herself love him as she had wanted to from the beginning . . . Mama, Edward, the whole structure of her upbringing, conscience, conduct and the proposed bill for the punishment of adultery – all were forgotten.

As Rosie had said, everything was so simple when she made no difficulties. She took the Rao in her arms. Neither of them thought again of patronage, revenge, humiliation, respect or conduct.

Living in the hiatus of bliss which is the lover's special climate, Florence and the Rao gave no heed to the rest of the world – that is, to Rosie or the ladies downstairs. Anything farther afield than the Rani's island did not exist for them. As time went by, and Florence did not reappear among them, and Rosie remained uncommunicative as to the true state of affairs, the ladies whispered together when the children were out of earshot. That *poor* little Mrs Mulgrove, they said, she must be having a terrible time . . . He had never kept any of them there so long. Whatever could he see in her? She was always so mousy . . . But mousy or not, they said, still waters run deep . . . They began to think that perhaps, after all, Florence was not quite what she seemed. One and all felt slighted.

Great comfort was derived from Rosie's downfall. At last she had met her come-uppance. It had been impossible from the start, having her, a servant girl, queening it over them as Rani. If such a situation must be accepted, then it would be far more suitable with Florence. After all, she was the Honourable . . . she knew how to behave. As one, they now turned Rosie out of the palace. Not that this troubled Rosie – she had other cares. What was going on upstairs – that was worrying, now. She feared the Rao's infatuation was stronger than she had thought. Miss Florence, too, seemed strangely changed. Things weren't turning out at all as she had expected. Well . . . give them time.

Rosie took some cushions and settled herself into an abandoned marble pavilion on the edge of the jungle. In her new loneliness she adopted a small furry animal of singular ugliness. She had found it lying beside a bamboo thicket. It was squeaking pathetically and she supposed its mother had met with an accident. It was a rabbity creature, with beady eyes and sharp tusky teeth of an unprepossessing orange colour. But it held nuts, or fruits, in its tiny paws in a most winning fashion, eating with noisy gusto, falling on its food with such relish it could be heard guzzling at quite a distance. Soon Rosie was besotted on it. She named it Snuggles. Unconsciously, here on this remote island, Rosie was conforming to the classical tradition of lonely prisoners and found herself consoled by a rat. (It was, in fact, a *Rhizomys pruinosus*, or bamboo rat, but there was no one to tell her so.) She made him a cradle out of an empty gourd which she lined with a piece of silk torn from one of her numerous saris. There was a time, she thought sadly, when the Rao had showered her with such gifts. She could not bear to think of him up there with Miss Florence, alone together in the painted room where once . . .

Rosie did not like the way things were going, not at all she didn't, watching at night the faint blur of two entwined figures swaying in the silver swing she had come to regard as her own. But hanging over Snuggles's crib, noting every furry perfection, the pink bud-like ears and the infinitesimal sandy lashes closed over those beady bright eyes as he slumbered so innocently, she felt comforted. Sometimes he would squeak in his sleep, (he slept beside her), and she would wake, fearful that he was ailing. But it was just some jungly nightmares he could not share, so she patted him and he grunted and nestled down contentedly in the crimson-and-gold gauze.

The rains had broken, drumming down on the marble rooftops, smashing the leaves, choking the earth and turning the island to a swamp. In the mirrored hall, the ladies sat sulking, swallowing the bitter pill of rejection. Over and over again they recalled with the loudest condemnation the Rao's favours. But now, deprived of them, they sat in judgment on Florence. There was no more reason to wear the beautiful saris they had once rebelled against, although there was no denying they were becoming, so only a few ladies returned to their petticoats and corsets. But all of them continued to wear as many jewels as the Rao had left them. He had sent for quite a quantity for Florence's benefit, but since his original generosity had been prodigious, the ladies were still lavishly ornamented and derived a certain solace from their splendours. There was no more reason to keep the children cooped up in the taikhana, since the lovers remained sequestered upstairs. So the children surged about the Hall of the Peacocks, straining their mothers' already frayed nerves sadly when they kept on asking for Uncle Rao to come and play with them.

'Uncle Rao has other things to do. Now be quiet and stop

fidgeting,' was the usual reply, so the children were mystified and bored and more fidgety than ever, since they were forbidden to go anywhere except on the northern side of the palace. From there, they ran no risk of catching sight of the lovers on the rooftop and asking questions which might have been very awkward to answer.

Rosie still spent most of her time with Snuggles in the garden pavilion. The rain lashed down, but they were well sheltered. It was clear the little creature returned Rosie's affection and he would sit up on his haunches, staring at her sentimentally, occasionally squeaking, and trotting off into the jungle to return busily with a grub or a mangled lizard, token of love, which he would lay at her feet, watching anxiously to see if she was pleased. Had she known it, he was behaving very much as the Rao was with Florence.

To pass the time, Rosie now made Snuggles a little gold paper crown and invited the children to a coronation ceremony in which he was to be crowned king of the jungle. Rosie was catching up on the games and toys her childhood had been denied. The children were delighted. The ceremony went off very well, everybody making obeisance before the bamboo rat as he sat in state on the poop of the grounded state barge. The Rao, on one of his rare descents to earth from the paradise of Florence's embrace, had learned of the impending ceremony and seemed interested. He was, in fact, thankful that Rosie's mind was elsewhere. There had been a moment when he feared she might be tiresome – she was of such a very impetuous nature. In gratitude, he charged the children to present Snuggles with one of his heavy gold ankle bracelets. The bamboo rat wore it as a belt. It fitted very nicely and he did not seem to mind at all; in fact, he seemed proud. He was a singularly intelligent little thing and Rosie had every reason to

be grateful to Providence for sending her this unlikely
companion to lessen her loneliness.

Once Florence had accepted the shattering fact of her union
with the Rao Jagnabad, she behaved entirely according to the
tradition of her kind. She now saw herself as the mother of his
children. Not an echo of the shrieks and groans that had so
tormented her at Shepheard's Hotel remained to cloud the
prospect of some seraphic toffee-coloured infant to crown their
bliss. She even imagined it in the Honiton lace christening
robes worn by succeeding generations of her family. And of
course she yearned to know what her lover had looked like as a
child.

'Tell me about your childhood, Presence,' she said fondly,
though still employing the obsequious address of the traditional
zenana – wife. 'You must have been such a handsome child,'
she went on and the Rao did not contradict her. Florence
imagined the little brown boy scampering through the sun-
slashed courtyards of his mother's palace. Fondly she smoothed
back a lock of blue-black hair that fell across his face. 'My
black, black sheep,' she said tenderly, thinking without a qualm
of his late wicked behaviour. 'I expect they all spoiled you
terribly in the palace, didn't they?'

'What palace, my angel?' asked the Rao absently. He was
frowning, the proud head bent intently over a number of
jewelled toe rings which he was arranging and rearranging on
Florence's already braceleted feet, which she now assiduously
tinted with henna.

'Your mother's palace – when you were little,' replied
Florence, who was languidly employing an ivory-and-ebony
inlaid back scratcher; and enjoying this practice which once
would have aroused her condemnation. She was still picturing
all the colour and beauty and exoticism of her lover's

background – so different from her own cramped nursery in the London house where she and her brother George had been under Nanny Blodgett's iron rule.

The Rao laughed – rather defiantly, she thought. His face hardened. It was the snarling tiger's mask once more.

'No,' he said, 'no, for to speak truth, my Florensse, there is never palace as born place, no zenana, no mother, no father . . . I wish that I tell you all. You will listen. I am not Rao. I am lost boy, in the year of cholera. I sleep in the bazaars. I am hungry. The Mission fathers take me in school and give me food. I eat much. I learn also. I go to Arungabad. Soon I become secretary to a Mirza – a prince. Then another. Then I please a beautiful Begum and it is trouble with her husband. I run away and I am kitmaghar – butler – in English house in Calcutta. I speak English good. I listen much. I study. Then I please a memsahib and there is much trouble . . . I go quick to Rajputana and the Maharaja makes me secretary. He trusts me. We hunt tiger. I kill many. I am Nine Tiger Man. I make the Maharaja proud. I kill his enemies too. He loves me. He has no son and he adopting me soon. Much jealous people everywhere, but now I am Rao. The Maharaja is loyal with English. In his palace come many powerful sahibs. We hunt together. We are friends. The Maharaja sends me to England so to fight for lands the sahibs steal. I try – I try. I do not get. I do not see the great Queen Sahib. The English sahibs smile and promise me much thing, and I smile and I believe. But I get nothing. I do not get the memsahibs . . . but they also smile and promise me much . . . I am sad. I am angry. Then I come to your most honoured mother's house. She is noble, working much to help me, but it is of uselessness.' He shook his head forlornly. The tiger had vanished, to be replaced by an orphan boy. Florence's heart was wrung.

'My poor precious,' she murmured dotingly, aching with love and longing to make it all up to him. The Rao took a slow consoling pull at his hookah before continuing. Then, gloomily, he said, 'It is failure, I am failed. I must return to Maharaja and tell. I am grievous . . . Then I see you look at me, Florensse, you are like angel, so silver. I want you. I want to love you much. But I cannot say to you this. I am Hindu man. I am not good for memsahibs . . . And then . . .' He came to a halt, remembering his sense of loneliness, of failure and of the house party's barely concealed attitude of patronage, so easily discernible beneath all the flattery. And how, in a mood of humiliation and resentment, he had gone into his room and there found Rosie – and with her, forgetfulness.

It would not do to tell Florence that. She could not be expected to understand. She was, after all, a memsahib, however angelic. But Florence was looking at him, all love and softness and understanding.

'And then . . . ?' she prompted him. 'Then, my darling, tell me why you did not answer my letter? Did you think it unwomanly of me? I waited all next day for you to speak, but you never even looked in my direction . . . I was so unhappy . . . so humiliated. Tell me, why did you go away like that, without speaking?'

The Rao looked at her blankly. 'I am not understanding. What letter? Why you are sad for what I do? I do wrong, my Florensse, my Indrani ?'

She told him of the letter, of what it had cost her to write it, of her shame and despair. 'So you see,' she said, 'it was I who was humiliated, you who did not want my love! Oh Presence! Oh pet!' she ended, love and reproach struggling in her soul.

But seeing such bewilderment and despair written on the Rao's face, she realized he had never received her letter. Suddenly Rosie's perfidy was apparent. The whole mystifying business was clear. So that was why he had not spoken! Rosie had suppressed the letter and lied to her, slyly, abominably . . . Florence was, as the Rao believed, of an angelic nature and still limpid in her innocence, so she had not yet gauged the degree of Rosie's perfidy. She could not imagine that Rosie had not only suppressed her letter, but taken advantage of the occasion to steal him away from her and spend the whole night – two nights, more precisely – in his arms.

All the same, the most disquieting suspicions were nagging at her. She had to admit that they had been there, lying dormant, purposely ignored, at the back of her mind ever since she had witnessed that extraordinary meeting between the Rao and Rosie when he had first arrived on the island. Rosie had behaved in such a strangely forward manner, singing that song. Then by the way they spoke together it seemed impossible to deny they must have known each other before. But she had been too proud – too cowardly – to question Rosie. She had not allowed herself to think of it. It was too upsetting. But now she knew. Her own maid – and at Bogwood! It had been terrible enough to endure the anguish caused by what had happened here with all the other ladies and Rosie putting on airs as the favourite . . . but this was too much!

Yet did any of it really matter? Not any more. Not when she knew such happiness as now. She lay with her head on the Rao's shoulder, wishing he would not wear quite so many jewels, for they scratched painfully. There was hardly an inch of his tunic that was not studded with pearls, or embroidered stiff with gold thread, while the huge uncut emeralds of his necklace felt like pebbles under her cheek. But that was of no account either, she thought, clasped in his arms and, in the manner of her generation, dissolved in tears of bliss.

Since the Rao had not been brought up in mid-Victorian England, he was quite unaware that tears were then accepted as an expression of joy as much as of sorrow.

He bent over Florence anxiously, 'My pearl, my soul,' he murmured tenderly, 'why crying? Why sad? You are angry Rosee is loving me at Bogwood?'

He too had now realized Rosie's perfidy and his anger flared up. He would kill her! But then, on second thoughts, he felt inclined to make allowances, for he recalled the furious hunger which had possessed them both that night. There had been little time for her to give him Florence's letter, or for him to read it, either. And then, too, he knew why Rosie snatched at pleasures. Like himself, she had been an orphan, poor and patronized. Adventures, risks, the power of her body – these were her only means of obtaining anything from life, as once they had been for him. Still, he was very angry with her, very, very angry. She had delayed his coming together with Florence, his adored, his angel, his Queen of Paradise.

'Rosie was doing a wickedness,' he said. 'Do not cry, my pearl . . . See, I go now to kill her quick.'

He picked up the dagger that lay beside them and began to unclasp Florence's arms. But when she spoke to him of mercy and forgiveness, (and how inconvenient it would be if Rosie was no longer there to run errands and wait on them), he relented – with a certain carefully dissimulated alacrity, however, for he still thought Rosie a lovely creature. She was generous in her ways. He had enjoyed her – enjoyed her greatly . . . Perhaps, who could tell – perhaps it would be better to keep Rosie at hand? Yes. He would not kill her, though she must be taught a lesson. If he were to slice off the tip of her nose, now, or perhaps one breast? That would punish her. But then, it would quite spoil her looks, too. It would be better to show mercy, in Florence's Christian memsahib way.

Putting down the dagger, he said: 'I do not kill Rosee. I beat her.' But all the same, he would never forgive her for cheating him of one single hour of Florence's wonderful love. He would thrash her within an inch of her life. He would drag her round the courtyard by the hair of her head . . . and he might even threaten to throw her to the crocodiles. He must make sure she understood the enormity of her crime. But first he wanted to love Florence, beautiful, angelic, pearly-pure Florence, as he had never loved even Rosie. He wanted to make it up to her, to himself too, for all those wasted hours at Bogwood – hours when they might have been together, but of which Fate, or rather Rosie, had cheated them.

'It is getting night,' he said. 'We go to the terrace.' He led the doting Florence out on to the rooftop where the first stars were glittering low over the surrounding jungle, and the last, late, green parrots were winging homewards in the shadowy dusk.

Hours later, not wasted hours, however, when the declining moon had paled in a radiant morning sky and a breeze was crisping the lake, they heard footsteps on the stairs.

Rosie stood before them, shading her eyes against the light. The Rao sprang up furiously. He had given orders that no one was ever to come up to the terrace when he and Florence were there. Gone were the days when he would clap his hands and order half a dozen of the memsahibs upstairs to distract him as he and Rosie sported there. How dared she! How dared she stand there, staring at them! He had better kill her after all. He reached for his dagger, his eyes murderous. Rosie did not flinch.

'A messenger has rowed over from the mainland. Your Maharaja is back and he is asking for you and the ladies. The messenger is in the courtyard . . . My word, I wouldn't be in your shoes for anything!' she shot at him, as she clattered down the stairs.

IX

The messenger had arrived in a small raft-like canoe – a catamaran. Now it was moored below the line of trumpeting elephants, the boatman sitting in it, munching a water melon. The man he had brought across was none other than the Chamberlain, one of the Maharaja's most confidential advisers and generally entrusted with missions of a delicate nature. Peeping through the lattices, harem-fashion, the ladies watched the two men pacing up and down the terrace above the landing stage. They were talking together earnestly. The Chamberlain, a bilious-looking man, was gesticulating, laying about with an imaginary sword to emphasize his arguments, while the Rao listened with his usual air of haughty impassivity. He was in undress. That is, he had gone straight down from the terrace and was still in the loose caftan and small round embroidered velvet cap he wore at night. Round his waist a brilliant gold-spangled muslin scarf was wound and, as always, his jade- and-ruby handled dagger was thrust into its folds. His feet were bare; narrow and brown and beautiful, they paced the scorching marble paving, apparently insensible to the heat it radiated.

Gazing down on him from the roof, Florence felt her passion quite overwhelming. How handsome, how splendid, how powerful he was, her Nine Tiger Man, standing there in the blaze of the morning sun. How strangely he had come into her life and now was all of it. Everything about her was changed now. Through her love for him she had come to love the East – India. She no longer found it cruel, or uncomfortable, or even dirty . . . The heat, the insects, the peculiar foods and those temple carvings and pictures she had thought so shocking when Edward had ventured to show her any, all seemed entirely natural now, for she saw them through the Rao's eyes which had become her own.

It no longer seemed in the least odd to be listening to those burning Oriental similes where the beloved's charms were catalogued in detail. The stomach, for example, had always seemed to Florence something indelicate, a portion of her anatomy never mentioned; at best some internal mechanism which dealt with food. Now she found it was one of her major attractions. The Oriental took an erotic, aesthetic view of the stomach, or belly, dwelling on its roundness, whiteness, softness . . . It was clearly something to be admired, worshipped even . . . In the words of Solomon's Song: 'Thy navel is like a round goblet which wanteth not liquor; thy belly is like an heap of wheat set about with lilies.' But then Florence had not been allowed to read the Old Testament, so that when Jagnabad, spending hours in rapt contemplation, murmured the words of some long-dead Hindu poet – 'She, whose smooth silver belly recalls the full moon' – Florence found it strangely pleasing and made no invidious comparisons as to literary style.

At sunset the Rao would lean over the marble balustrade and call the monkeys with a curious wild cry. They would come scampering to him, hurtling round, swarming on to the terrace, chattering and grabbing, swinging themselves up on to his shoulder, balancing on his head, picking at the jewels in his turban, searching intently in his hair and beard . . . invading hordes that were now, somehow, welcome guests. Florence had not liked the monkeys at first . . . they gave her the creeps, with their snatching hands and nearly human faces. But Rosie had always laughed and welcomed them and fed them. 'Come on! Look sharp! It's Jacko'clock,' she would say as the sun sank behind the far hills. And she sent Florence, or any other of the memsahibs who were then her slaves, to fetch nuts and fruit. 'Jacko'clock' was her great joke and she laughed uproariously, trying to explain it to the Rao, telling him all monkeys were 'Jackoes' to her, remembering the Italian organ grinders and their dressed-up little monkeys that occasionally appeared at the village fairs, both of them grinning anxiously for pennies. They were pennies Rosie never had to give them, then. So now she tried to make it up, with handful after handful of nuts and bananas which she kept Mrs Pettifer peeling by the dozen. The Jackoes were perfectly able to peel their bananas for themselves, but Rosie, (and the Rao), enjoyed watching Mrs Pettifer's face when she was compelled to wait on the apes.

Now, Florence herself waited on them gladly. She too had come to love 'Jacko'clock', when in the soft golden afterglow the monkeys answered the Rao's call in their hundreds. 'Sweet creatures,' said Florence, feeling a warmth so seldom experienced by the hostess of such hungry, pressing guests. She was even a little jealous: a current of sympathy seemed to flow between the monkeys and her lover.

'I am monkey boy in Temple once,' he had said, but he did not enlarge on this period of his life. She supposed he had been in charge of their food and welfare. In any case, these wild monkeys responded to his call with the same trust as no doubt the sacred Temple creatures had once shown.

All the same, Florence felt relieved there were no snakes on the island. Cobras, rat snakes, tree snakes, sea snakes, or the dreaded krait . . . she really did not think her love could have survived seeing the cobras writhing across the terrace and coiling round, even if it was the Rao who charmed them. But all the rest of India she saw as if through his own eyes, and she loved it unquestioningly. As for the great encroaching green jungle tides that had once seemed to envelop her, to reach out and clutch her, they were now only leaves which shaded her at noon, or fragrant thickets scenting the breeze that cooled her so deliciously at evening. And if, as she had once feared, they had a life of their own, then it was part of some limitless kingdom where vegetal life, animal life, human life, and her own and the Rao's too, were all merged; all part of some vast sensuous whole.

Yet this rich kingdom of the senses, so exuberant in its life force, could still be threatened, or at least shadowed, by thoughts of Bogwood and the exigencies of civilization. She sighed. What lay before them – she and the Rao – in their new life together? She supposed they would have to return to the mainland one day. She would like to have sent all the rest of the women packing and remained on the island alone with the Rao forever. But that she knew would be impossible. First, there was Edward. How was he going to take this? How was he going to behave when she told him she could never, never return to him – that she belonged to another? . . . Belonged: it was a word of many interpretations. Edward was her husband, yet had she ever really belonged to him? Not as she now belonged to the Rao. Then there was Rosie and all the other ladies: they too had, in a sense, belonged to the Rao . . . But it had become a world where only he and she existed. She could no longer imagine a day or an hour of life without him. They were one. One – and nothing and nobody must ever come between them. Nothing else counted. Not even the dreadful explanations to Edward or Mama.

She found herself wondering whether, on returning to the mainland, she might perhaps learn of Edward's untimely (but most convenient) end, defending the British Raj. Widowhood: she saw herself draped in a black sari – oddly, she no longer pictured herself mourning even Edward in anything but a sari. From the Rao she had learned much about Hindu beliefs and customs, admitting them indiscriminately. Still, perhaps not quite to the point of admitting suttee – the widow's immolation on a burning pyre. And certainly not for Edward. Her heart lifted at the thought of being able to return to the Rani's island, (after the briefest period of mourning), as the new Rani – wife of the Rao Jagnabad. Sole wife, naturally, for polygamy, although one of the cornerstones of Indian family life, was not something to which she had yet applied her mind. At present the question had not arisen, the Rao being, in his infatuation, as

single-minded as she was. She was quite contented to be, in the
graceful Indian phrase, 'the curtain-wife of affection.'
Nevertheless, she sometimes luxuriated in the prospect of a
widowhood which would enable her to be his undisputed, legal
wife. And then, realizing the implications of this desire, she put
it from her firmly. If indeed Edward had met his death, it would
have been at the hand of a mutineer – a Hindu – one of her
lover's own race. How distressing it all was . . . Still, there was
no denying that Edward's demise would simplify matters
greatly.

From her exile in the abandoned pavilion, Rosie too watched
the Rao longingly. But she was a realist. She knew that life on
the island must come to an end soon for all of them. Since she
was no longer the favourite, the sooner they returned to the
mainland, the better she would be pleased. She was already
planning to take Snuggles with her, and had been contriving a
travelling basket for him made out of woven leaves. Snuggles
watched her sharply. She fancied he was aware of the
approaching move and disapproved. But he only grunted when
she told him about the splendours of the Chandni Chowk; and
tusked away at the bamboo stems as if to eat his fill before
leaving.

Through the fretted leaves Rosie could see the Rao and his
visitor pacing up and down the terrace above the landing-stage.
There was something particularly savage – yes, really tiger-like,
she thought – in the way the Rao moved. She sensed a growing
tension in the air. There seemed to be an argument. The Rao
moved his head with that same proud, restive movement Rosie
had first remarked when she watched him through the
conservatory at Bogwood. Then, he had been the centrepiece of
a formal dinner table, bowing, receiving homage and returning
the toasts of his well-wishers. Now, a mounting sense of drama,

of doom, overcame the peaceful scene where butterflies hovered over the roses and the talkers paced the garden side by side; and the tiny striped squirrels frisked about their feet, chattering impudently.

As Rosie watched, the peaceful image was shattered. The Chamberlain raised one hand as if invoking his gods and then, with a sweep, drew his sword halfway from its scabbard. His face, Rosie saw, was contorted with rage.

At the same moment, the Rao's brown jewelled hand flashed out and the jade-handled dagger plunged deep into the Chamberlain's flesh, felling him to the ground. The Rao jerked his dagger free. The Chamberlain now began to thrash about, uttering a series of terrible, monotonous screams that recalled to the shuddering Florence the gruesome mechanics of Tippoo's Tiger and the Missionary which had upset her so long ago in Leadenhall Street. To the listening women, it seemed the screams would never stop. He is overwound, thought Florence hysterically, confusing the dying Chamberlain with the mechanical missionary. But at last he lay quite still, quite silent.

The Rao had been watching him stonily. Now, with the lightning movement of the hunter falling on his prey, he turned and sprang at the boatman who was running up the steps towards the fallen Chamberlain. But the boatman dodged, doubled back to his boat, slashed the mooring rope and was off, paddling furiously for the mainland. The Rao walked back slowly and passed the body of the Chamberlain without so much as a glance. From their different vantage points, behind the lattices, from the rooftop, or among the leaves, his entire zenana had watched the drama in stricken silence. They did not know what it signified, but a new and even more terrifying aspect of the Rao's nature was now revealed. They saw all that violence and ruthlessness which they had only glimpsed before, and which had also been an unavowed, but fatal attraction. Now they knew why he was known as the Nine Tiger Man. They had seen the killer kill.

For a long while, it seemed, the Rao stood staring fixedly across the lake towards the mainland. Then he turned and walked towards the palace, calling for the Tibetans. They too must have been watching close by, for they came trotting out on the instant. The Rao pointed to the corpse and issued some brief command. The phantoms prostrated themselves while the Rao carefully wiped his dagger on the old woman's rags. Then, with a certain air of good humour, he kicked them to their feet. They shuffled back into the jungle, dragging the Chamberlain's body after them. A pool of blood was congealing on the white marble paving and the squirrels darted close, curious to investigate. Then, finding this was nothing for them, they scampered away, also making for the jungle's depth.

The Rao bounded up the stairway to where he had left Florence on the rooftop. She was standing by the low marble balustrade as if herself turned to stone. He threw himself at her feet, covering them with kisses. This was not a gesture of repentance. He was not asking her forgiveness for what he had done, for indeed, he had no sense of guilt. He was merely expressing the profound love he felt for her – an emotion he had never felt for any other woman.

'Florensse – my angel Florensse, my moon-pearl,' he said dreamily, pulling her down beside him on the cushions.

Florence, who was still faint with terror at the scenes he had just witnessed, sank down beside him, unable to speak. But she felt no revulsion, no fear. Her love for him remained unchanged. However, murder was not something that could be ignored altogether. It called for some explanation. No doubt there was a good reason for such violence. But before she could question her lover, he had forestalled her.

What he had to tell was worse – far worse than anything Florence had just seen, or could have imagined.

The Chamberlain had come to fetch the Rao back, for the Maharaja had returned to his kingdom sooner than was expected and was asking for his regent before he had dismounted. Moreover, he was accompanied by two sahibs appointed by the British to serve as his advisers. One of them was an army officer. The other was a civilian, the Sahib Mulgrove. Since his wife was among the memsahibs whom the Maharaja was sheltering, it had seemed most suitable he should be sent to arrange for their return to Azampur. The revolt had not taken hold there. Save for a few tentative risings in outlying areas which had been repressed, things were now quite calm. Delhi had fallen, the rebel princes had been shot out of hand and the old King was awaiting trial. Although heavy fighting continued across the country, and Lucknow was still besieged, the tide had at last turned. All this was most gratifying to the Maharaja and his barons who had remained staunchly loyal to the British Raj, and had been through some uneasy moments before Delhi was once more in British hands.

Now returned to his own lands, the Maharaja wished to discuss the conduct of his kingdom with the Rao. Why was he absent? For how long had he been absent? Where was he? Were all the memsahibs in good health? Something in his courtiers' manner now aroused the Maharaja's suspicions that all was not well. Under threat of torture the courtiers soon revealed the whole affair.

They had long been jealous of the Rao. Now, foreseeing his downfall, they did not hesitate to denounce him. With unctuous zeal they told how he had arrived on the Rani's island, dismissed them all and held court there, sole ruler of a zenana composed exclusively of the memsahibs. Of how he had rifled the palace treasury of its finest jewels to adorn his favourites and had been remaining there in isolation for three moons or more, having instructed the palace personnel, on pain of death, not to approach the island before he sent up a signal rocket.

On learning this, the Maharaja was seized with apoplexy, so that the Royal physicians despaired of his life. However, he rallied. Now, faced with this deplorable situation, he prepared to make what amends he could. He knew of and indeed sympathized with his adopted son's sense of bitterness and injustice regarding the failure of his mission in London. But to betray a sacred trust and the laws of hospitality, to dishonour honoured guests, was no way to behave. However much resentment the Rao felt, he had now brought disgrace on every one concerned: on the memsahibs, on himself as the Maharaja's regent and on the Maharaja, his father by adoption, who had sworn by the most solemn oaths to protect the memsahibs entrusted to his care. Never again could a Rajput hold up his head, or look an Englishman in the eyes. His noble friends the sahibs, to whom he had given his word, would now find they too were dishonoured, and by his own heir, in his own palace, in the zenana of his grandmother, the revered Rani.

The Maharaja, said the Chamberlain, had rolled on the ground in paroxysms of rage and sliced off the heads of several slaves before he could be calmed . . . In circumstances such as the memsahibs now found themselves, the Chamberlain said, Rajput women would of course have run on the sword. Only death could cleanse dishonour. But the memsahibs were so different . . .

Still, amends would have to be made. Thus the Maharaja now requested the immediate return of His Highness the Rao Jagnabad. He was to present himself at the Palace without delay. The memsahibs would be fetched later, in time to be present at the Rao's trial. If he were to remain true to his oath, said the Court, the Maharaja would be compelled to decapitate the Rao. He should strike the fatal blow using the tulwar of his ancestors, before the assembled army and all the highest in the realm, while his British advisers and the memsahibs should be placed in the front rank, as the protocol and their sufferings demanded. Only thus could they be in any measure avenged. Only thus could their husbands, Queen Victoria, and indeed the whole British people to whom he had sworn allegiance, know that the Maharaja and his Court had done all that lay in their power to right so terrible a wrong.

'This is what the Chamberlain came to tell you?' asked Florence, grown haggard at the horror of their situation. Edward here, on the mainland – the Rao threatened – she fought back her tears.

The Rao took her in his arms, 'Yes, he is angry that I do not go back quick. I say no. I follow. First I say, I must love you once more. He is angry again. I kill him. It is finish . . . Now we love and say goodbye . . .' He bent over Florence, staring deep into her horror-struck eyes, his dark, serpent-like locks falling round her as they strained close.

Goodbye? But they were to be together for evermore! Panic gripped Florence. Thoughts of Edward, Mama, divorce, or ever being able to live happy ever after with the Rao now vanished. Only one thing counted. The Rao's life. How to save him from the Maharaja's sword? Somehow he must escape. He must swim over to the farther shores of the lake and make his way to the coast – to the North West Frontier – anywhere, beyond the confines of Rajputana. Later she would join him . . . She would have to face Edward alone . . . but now, there was no time to lose. Soon the boats would be coming over from the mainland . . . He must go now – this minute!

She began outlining her plan, wringing her hands distractedly, as she spoke. The Rao had never seen her so determined. This was no longer the docile milky miss he had hardly dared to touch. He had brought her to life in his arms, fired her with the heat of his passion and now she was this masterful stranger. Shock, bewilderment and disappointment too, were written across his face.

'But Florensse, my angel, it is finish. I must to go back! You do not understand? First we love together once more . . . Come Florensse . . . '

Now it was Florence's turn to stare in astonishment. She could not imagine that this ruthless fighter, this daemonic man, could abandon himself so fatalistically to their parting, or that he could think of lovemaking at such a moment.

'You don't want to escape? You are going to let them separate us? No, I don't understand!'

Florence, the adoring, faced him, her features positively distorted, beating against him with her fragile braceleted hands.

'Listen to me!' she shouted, shrewish in her desperation. 'You cannot go back! You cannot stay here! Are you mad? Go now, or they will hunt you down. I will find a way to join you later. But go – go now.'

The Rao caught her beating hands and held them still. 'No, my pearl, no, Florensse angel, I go back. It is better I go in honour to my master. If he kill me, I die happy, after what happens here.' He smiled his strange, sweet and childlike smile. Holding Florence's hands up against the light, he told her for the hundredth time that they were like alabaster and he could see the sun through them.

But Florence was of the West. This was no time for dalliance. She snatched her hands away. Besides, to talk of dying happy was rubbishy talk. No death by violence could be a happy one. Death was, to her, an ending, whereas to the East it was a beginning – the doorway to Preta Loka, the world of the departed, a nebulous world of waiting, where the soul remains till it is reborn, in whatever form or condition its Karma decrees. Florence knew nothing about all this. Rao had never spoken of it to her, so the basic Hindu belief in reincarnation, the transition from a life to another life through the moment of death was quite incomprehensible to her.

'And me? You are going to leave me to Edward? Is that how you love me?' She was shrieking now. 'If you loved me you would want to be saved – you would want us to be together always. You would swim across to the far shore . . . they would never catch up with you there. I could tell them you had killed yourself – no, that the Chamberlain had killed you . . .'she was becoming incoherent now, sobbing hysterically.

The Rao smiled tenderly. He preferred her like that: it was more womanly than her former masterful fury.

He pointed down to the lake. 'You think the crocodiles let me swim safe? No, my Florensse, my little Memsahib Hookah-berdah, it is finish. We wait here, we love once more and then I go back honourable to Maharaja's sword. I am Rao Jagnabad, not poor runaway boy. I not cry Aman! and asking mercy.'

Florence felt a tide of hatred sweep over her. Hatred for fate that played this cruel trick, snatching away her love; her whole life. Hatred for the might of the Maharaja that would trap the Rao and perhaps put him to death before her eyes. Above all, she hated the unassailable, incomprehensible masculine pride of her lover. A scarlet tide of violence seemed to flood through her, blinding her, choking her. The Rao's arms were round her and he was pulling her down beside him on the silver swing. As he pressed her closer, all love, all furious desire, her hand closed over the dagger at his waist. Her face met his kisses at the same moment that her hand forced the dagger deep into his side. The scarlet tides that flooded across her mind were spreading over the Rao's body as it slid sideways from the swing and lay in a pool of blood. His eyes were open, but he did not seem to see Florence as she leaned over him, her face lit by a curious elation.

Now the Maharaja would never have him . . . nor the crocodiles . . . nor any other woman. He was hers – all hers. She possessed him entirely. Dead lovers are faithful.

The dark, slanted, inscrutable eyes slowly looked up. He smiled, but there was nothing childlike in this last smile. It was the faint, but unmistakable, snarl of the Tiger which so many women had found irresistible. He was not dying in honour, not dying like Sardanapaulus, of his own choice and surrounded by frenzied concubines. No – the Nine Tiger Man was dying by the hand of a memsahib . . .

'Ah Florensse . . . you love too strong,' he whispered. And died.

Florence was sitting by the Rao's body, keeping off the flies with the peacock fan of Majesty when, later, Rosie and the rest of the women ventured out. The evening sun beat down on her bare head, but she did not seem to feel it. The Rao's powerful form was stretched along the marble floor and his head lay on her knees. His face looked calm and happy. Except for the dagger which was still plunged up to the hilt in his flesh, he might have been sleeping the tired but triumphant sleep of a lover. Close by, the silver swing dangled to and fro in the breeze that was now stirring in the treetops. Soon it would be the hour the Rao had loved best, the hour when he called to the monkeys, 'Jacko'clock', the hour when the sky turned lemon and the parakeets flashed homeward across the lake, emerald in a golden setting. It was the hour when he had liked to sit in the swing with one or other of his favourites, this splendid, wicked man who now lay cold at their feet.

None of the women spoke, but they moved closer on tiptoe. At last Mrs Pettifer broke the silence. Putting a motherly arm round Florence she tried to raise her. 'You poor brave girl,' she said. 'You killed him – the wretch! . . . You suffered too much. We all understand . . . but now it is over. You must try to forget . . .'

They led Florence downstairs, full of commiseration for what she had been through, full of admiration for her brave deed. She had rid the world of a monster, they said. She was a real heroine! Not one of them cared to show regret for the Rao's death. It would not do. They must remember they were helpless victims of his lust and Mrs Mulgrove, stabbing him, had acted for all of them. They led her to the alcove she had occupied before the Rao had installed her beside him in the Rani's painted bedroom. Covering her with quilts, they left her to rest. She lay there, pale and composed, her eyes closed and looking, Rosie thought, more like a stone figure on a tomb than ever. She did not weep. They could not know that she was re-living, over and over again, the Rao's caresses, savouring again that world of delights she had known with him and that now no one could ever take from her. She would never have to share him, for dead lovers are faithful. The ladies, watching her anxiously, saw a smile pass across her drawn features. Poor little thing, they thought, she is dreaming. They tiptoed away, careful not to wake her.

Rosie was never one to cry over spilt milk. Seeing her lover lying there had been a shock. But he was dead and nothing would bring him back. In any case, she doubted he would ever have come back to her – not for any length of time, that is. Now her one idea was to reach the mainland as soon as possible. How much of their life on the Rani's island was known there, she could not tell, for only Florence knew what news the Chamberlain had brought and why the Rao had killed him – and also, the true reason why she, Florence, had murdered her lover. But Rosie had a shrewd idea there would have been a lot of trouble for him if he had returned to the Maharaja's court. And there would be even more trouble for all of them if it became known that Florence, a memsahib, had struck down the Rao.

'Now listen to me, all of you!' she shouted truculently. The ladies stopped their gabble, struck dumb by such impertinence.

'There will be trouble – a lot of trouble – if everything that has happened here comes out. Are you going to keep your mouths shut? Well – are you?' she said, looking round at the speechless, pasty-faced ladies.

'Things may go very bad for all of us – and the children – if you blab to the Maharaja how the Rao died. Whatever he did, he was the Maharaja's favourite. These foreigners see things different to us. We don't know how the war is going . . . we don't know where our gentlemen are . . . We'd better not talk or we shall find ourselves in Queer Street good and proper. Or do you want to blab it all out to your husbands? All about how you used to fight among yourselves to spend a night upstairs. Oh yes you did,' she went on, relishing the sight of the ladies, flushed and uncomfortable. 'I saw you – I watched how you began to enjoy yourselves. I don't blame you, neither . . . But then, you see, it's all according . . . I'm not married. I'm accountable to no one. I can do as I fancy. Now with you and Miss Florence, that's another thing altogether . . . You've got your precious husbands waiting for you . . . I don't think what Miss Florence has just gone and done, killing the Rao, should be told to anyone, no more than what you've been up to . . . I shan't talk if you don't. Well what do you say?'

The ladies said nothing, but they looked their meek acquiescence. 'That's that, then,' said Rosie, now firmly in the saddle, and taking the lead over Mrs Tollemache's head. 'Then we'd best get rid of the body before they find it and start asking questions.'

'But how?' faltered Mrs Tollemache, feeling the situation quite beyond her. Two murders in one day! Whatever next?

Rosie shot her a contemptuous glance. 'The lake don't tell tales,' she said. 'We'll shove him over the wall where it's deep . . . the crocodiles . . .' She stopped, thinking sickeningly of those snapping jaws mangling the body she had found so splendid. She forced herself not to think of the Rao as she had known him. Now he was only something they must get rid of as quickly as possible – a heavy packet.

'What if those Tibetans talk?' asked another lady fearfully. But Rosie had thought of that.'

'They'll keep quiet enough if we give them enough jewels,' she replied. 'You'd best go and fetch all you can at once,' she went on firmly. She had no intention of parting with any of her own and she watched the ladies hurrying off with complacency. She despised the whole lot. They didn't even put up a fight. Let them pay hush money for their precious virtue's sake – to the Tibetans – to her too, yes. Before she was through with them they'd have to part with even more. She was never going to want again, if she could help it. Neither want, nor work, in the sense of work as she'd known it at Bogwood. She meant to travel, to see more of the world. And then, there was little Snuggles. He must have the best of everything. Perhaps it would be wise to settle down somewhere nice and warm . . .

She came down to earth abruptly. First things first, my girl, she said to herself, remembering this was one of Mrs Maggot's favourite phrases, ruling the kitchen. The first thing to do now was to dispose of the Rao's body. It was decided that if they could drag it down the narrow stairway to the orange garden, they would be less likely to be seen by the Tibetans who generally remained on the far side of the palace, beside the landing stage.

'Now! Quick – get hold of his feet,' she said. As if galvanized, the women dragged and tugged at the body which had disgraced and delighted them. It was very heavy. They bumped it down the stairs, across the paved court where the nightingales sang in the orange trees, and on towards the jungle thickets leading to the little summer house hanging over the lake. It was here that Rosie had seen the crocodile emerge from the water below the window – and here it had plunged back into the depths in which it had its being.

The dreadful task upon which the ladies were embarked took a long time to accomplish. The body was as unwieldy as heavy, and as they dragged it by its feet, stiffened and clammy cold to the touch, they stumbled over their long skirts while the Rao's silken caftan caught on the thorns and creepers, as if the earth he had loved tried to hold him still. Above their heads, in the branches, the monkeys watched, swinging along beside them, uttering no sound and never coming close, as if they knew their friend no longer inhabited this clumsy object. The Rao's sash had twisted loose, but was still pinned to him by the dagger and trailed on the ground, tripping up the women as they staggered on.

At last the pavilion was reached, the crystal ornaments on the roof glittering out from among the dark leaves surrounding it. They heaved the body inside and tried to lift it over the windowsill. Time and again they strained to raise it, only to let it fall again, till the sweat trickled from their faces, blinding them. Their hair straggled down, giving them the appearance of so many Medusas.

But at last it was done. Head first and weighted by a sack of stones, the Nine Tiger Man's body slid down into the inky waters and sank almost without a ripple, leaving the lake as still and silent as before. It was all over, thought the women. All that was strange and terrible and beautiful had vanished with him, forever.

X

All that night the ladies waited tensely, expecting the arrival of a boat to fetch them back to the mainland to civilization, as it appeared when seen from the island. But no sound of oars broke the silence and nothing stirred on the inky stillness of the lake. The children became quite unmanageable, refusing to sleep, packing and repacking their Indian toys and fighting among themselves for possession of the rocking elephant. Moreover, they kept on asking for the Rao with maddening persistence. It appeared he had once promised he would take them to see a State execution where the prisoners – bad men, robbers and such – were trampled to death by the royal elephants. Both the Rao and the children seemed to regard this in the nature of a treat outing. Now the children were asking if Uncle Rao was going with them – would they see the elephants stamping on the robbers soon? Had Uncle Rao forgotten . . . ? At last their exasperated mothers boxed their ears and banished them to the taikhana for the rest of the night.

Rosie had prepared a travelling basket for Snuggles where, beneath the straw lining, she had concealed a large number of jewels; her own and those of the ladies who had handed them over without much fuss in the end. Rosie overfed her pet recklessly, for she wanted him to be somnolent on arrival at the Palace. It would be terrible, she thought, if he started nibbling at the Maharaja's grand ivory and pearl furniture and they tried to take him away from her . . . Rosie was not a motherly type, yet this odd little animal aroused every latent maternal instinct. He must have the best of everything and no one must lay a finger on him. Studying his whiskered snout, she thought it perfect. When his tiny intelligent eyes met hers with such understanding, she fancied she heard some kind of celestial Glockenspiel. She tucked him into his basket and he shifted uneasily, finding the jewels rather lumpy beneath the straw. But presently he settled philosophically, curled up and breathing stertorously, for he was bulged with bamboo shoots.

It was high noon before they heard the sound of drums. They rushed down to the landing stage to see, as once before, the State barge with its gilded tiger prow cleaving the water. Under the same awning that had once sheltered the Rao Jagnabad they saw again a group of turbaned figures. But now, as the boat came alongside, no fireworks figure sprang among them darting colour, jewels and force. Instead, a sober, sun-helmeted sahib stepped ashore with deliberation, followed by an officer in British uniform and a suite of Rajput nobles and guards.

Edward Mulgrove, accompanied by Captain Flashforth of the 49th Lancers, had come to fetch the ladies away.

As Edward climbed the steps he was searching for Florence's face among the women who stood there, primly buttoned and laced and looking, he thought, remarkably blooming, in spite of their dreadful ordeal. From the moment he had learned of events on the Rani's island he had feared for Florence's sanity. Such an ordeal was likely to have unhinged her mind. Rosie, that was different. He had few illusions about Rosie and at that moment caught sight of her, standing back a little from the rest, looking as pert as ever. Without surprise, he noticed she already had an eye for Captain Flashforth, who also seemed aware of her presence, for he was glancing at her covertly, fiddling with his moustaches and straightening his tunic.

The ladies crowded round, pouring out their tale of woe, so that it was some time before Edward could get a word in to ask after his wife. She was resting, they said – the heat had very much upset her lately . . . Yes, she was as well as could be expected . . . The Rao Jagnabad . . . ? A hush fell, the ladies looking – very naturally, Edward thought – embarrassed at the mention of their ravisher. No one had seen him since yesterday – since that shocking scene they had all witnessed – the murder of the Chamberlain . . . Oh yes! They'd seen it all . . . they didn't know what it meant, but it was too horrible. It was just there – exactly where Captain Flashforth was standing – yes, you could see the bloodstains on the marble . . . Really, they'd rather not talk about it . . . The Rajput nobles and the guards had come closer and were now looking from face to face trying to follow the gist of the conversation. Edward enlightened them briefly, at which every bearded face darkened threateningly and every hand was clasped on a sword . . . The atmosphere was charged with violence as they demanded the Rao's whereabouts, raging to bring him to justice. But Edward reminded them – justice was the Maharaja's. He would revenge the wrongs in his own time and manner. The ladies were now becoming so incoherent, babbling about crocodiles – something about an accident and the Rao having fallen in the lake – that Edward decided further questioning had better be postponed till they returned to the mainland. But he called Rosie to him and began enquiring about her mistress . . . Poor little Florence, he thought, I shall have to send in my resignation. It was hardly to be expected she would care to remain in India after what had happened.

'How did she take it?' he asked Rosie as he followed her towards the Rani's palace.

'Take what, sir?' asked Rosie innocently, preceding him through the great lacquered portals.

'Well, this business – this shocking business with the Rao Jagnabad.'

'You'd be surprised, sir. Much better than what you'd have thought,' Rosie answered, with truth. Edward shot her a glance. Had she too been one of the Rao's victims? It seemed likely, but Rosie's eyes were modestly downcast and revealed nothing. She was, in fact, wondering how Florence was going to take her husband's arrival on the island.

But when they reached the curtained alcove where Florence had been left, they found it empty. The cushions were strewn about and the coverlets in disorder. A heap of splendid saris was beside a jewelled hookah which Rosie recognized as the Rao's.

Poor creature, she must have crept upstairs and fetched it down, thought Rosie, understanding this longing for some link with the man she loved. Pinned to a cushion, in the classic manner of farewell letters, was a fold of paper addressed, 'To whom it may concern.' The writing was still elegant, in spite of being traced with a stump of charcoal. Edward seized it and read:

Do not search for me and do not mourn. By the time you read this I shall be beyond earthly cares. Tell my husband, Edward Mulgrove, I am sorry to cause him pain, but had I returned to him (even if he had wished me to do so) I could never again have been the wife he once knew. After what I have experienced here I am no longer the same woman. It is more fitting, now, that I should regard myself as the Rao's wife, and follow him in death in the Indian manner, for I am –

Here the letter broke off, as if the writer had been disturbed, or perhaps found any further ambiguities too difficult to muster. Or could no longer wait to join the man she had loved so ardently.

Sly – I always knew she was sly, thought Rosie, reading the letter as it dropped from Edward's hand. The statement it contained may have deceived the rest of the women, but did not at first altogether convince Edward. He was no fool and had already begun to suspect that perhaps, after all, the ladies' ordeal had not been quite so dreadful as they insisted. Though with Florence, of course, it was altogether different, he told himself firmly. First of all, she was his wife. Then, their honeymoon was hardly over . . . She was so young, so inexperienced. The shock must have been appalling. No doubt it had unhinged her mind. Yes, that was it. Now he saw just how her mind had worked.

She had been forced to submit to all sorts of unimaginable Eastern ways, until at last, in her anguish and shame, she had come to regard herself as the Rao's wife . . . In her confusion she believed herself to have become a moral outcast, unworthy of returning to either her lawful husband, or civilization. Poor little Florence . . . quite crazed by what she had gone through. A rush of pity overwhelmed Edward and he wept, for his was a truly generous nature.

Neither Florence's body nor that of the Rao Jagnabad were ever recovered from the lake. The crocodiles saw to that. However, a brief memorial service was held for Florence, the ladies sobbing unrestrainedly. Edward pronounced the funeral oration, dwelling on the virtues of charity, but he was careful not to make any allusions such as 'he who casts the first stone . . .'

He did not condemn Florence's suicide. He believed that for all her timidity, her revulsions, which he had not been able to overcome, she had, through her sufferings, become one with India and Indian customs as he, for all his academic knowledge, could never hope to do. And then, being a man, suttee, the voluntary immolation of bereaved wives, seemed to him a rather beautiful, if barbaric idea. There was no doubt civilization was destroying much that was fine.

'Suttee – the widow's sacrifice,' he said, addressing his snuffling audience, 'is an ancient Indian custom. Today we British condemn it, but we know it to be honourable in its intent. There can be many forms of suttee: by the funeral pyre, by poison, or as now, by water . . .'

The ladies thought it very odd that he should speak of his own wife as someone else's widow. 'Gone native! She'd gone native, that's all,' snorted Mrs Tollemache who was more profoundly shocked by the manner of little Mrs Mulgrove's death, and the extraordinary way in which Mr Mulgrove took it, than by anything else which had occurred.

Still, in the end, as so rarely in life, it all turned out for the best. The Rao was a wicked man and he perished. Yet Fate was kind. He, like Florence, had achieved his heart's desire. He had revenged himself on the British with his one-man Mutiny; and ruled in undisputed majesty over twenty-three memsahibs. Indeed, his revenge was even more complete than he had foreseen. For the memsahibs returned to their husbands dishonoured, and moreover, were dissatisfied for ever after with whatever marks of affection their magnanimous husbands were to bestow. And the Rao, having conscientiously worked out his revenge, found perfect love with Florence. She too had lived a sublime, if adulterous love, and she too had perished – but fortunately before custom could stale the infinite variety of her lover's caresses. True, she killed him and then took her own life. But this double crime saved a lot of trouble all round. The Maharaja was spared the painful moral obligation of putting his favourite to the sword. While Edward avoided the necessity of divorcing Florence, or even more unfortunate, of seeing her arraigned for murder.

Then, the children were removed from the enervating atmosphere of the island before it had undermined their characters. Being sent home at once, the rigorous atmosphere of British boarding schools soon expunged all memories of their happy tropic life. They had quickly learned not to remind their mothers of this time. Soon, they even forgot Uncle Rao . . . Alas! Some of the ladies were not so fortunate, for nature too revenged itself on them and they returned to their husbands in an unmistakably interesting condition. In spite of fevered recourse to a number of herbal concoctions by which their sympathetic ayahs guaranteed results, they were compelled to bear these reminders of their shame. Of course, since they were the victims of a satyr's lust, their husbands took the situation as well as could be expected. The sallow, unwanted infants were dispersed among a number of Indian orphanages run by missionaries of various denominations. No doubt they received the sort of upbringing calculated to quench any latent traces of immorality which they might have inherited from their sire.

To the end, some benign influence seemed to be at work, as if bent on repairing the disastrous course of events, for upon their return to cantonments, the ladies no longer bickered, or revealed those little sharp practices for which their sex is known. It was not so much that their shared trials had cemented the ties of friendship, as that each one now lived in terror of offending the other. All of them knew too much. All of them could have told tales of life in the zenana – tales which would have destroyed their husbands' confidence in their martyrdom and shattered the tragic halo they all wore so carefully. Thus the ladies resumed their interrupted lives in a rare spirit of goodwill, and their husbands marvelled at the change; while the Azampur cantonments enjoyed a reputation for harmony quite unique throughout British India.

Even for Edward, things turned out for the best in the end. First he went home on long leave, where he found it very difficult to explain matters to his mother-in-law. She flatly declined to believe that the Rao, her protégé, could so far have forgotten her Christian teachings as to have laid a finger on Florence, her own daughter and after staying at Bogwood too! Words failed her, she said, having thrashed the matter out loudly for several months. Later, Edward returned to India, becoming a high-ranking administrator, celebrated for his sympathetic dealings with the various states and native princes. It was as if the loss of his wife, in such particularly unusual circumstances too, had given him a special insight into the Indian character. Where a lesser man might have brooded, or turned against the nation as a whole, he flung himself into his work with disinterested devotion. There is a portrait of him, painted towards the end of his career, seated beside the young Rajput prince to whom he was Political Adviser. The Rani, courtiers and officers of state are grouped round in all their splendour. Edward does not cut much of a figure among them, for he wears elastic-sided boots and a heavy suit. His eyes are gentle, but there is, perhaps, something faintly resentful in his expression. Although it is as if he harboured a lingering grudge against life, rather than India, which in spite of all that had happened he continued to love. Married life, in particular, had disappointed him, but archaeology did not. Soon this passion quite overcame the emotions which Florence had briefly aroused. And when, in his seventieth year, riding in the Gujerat hills, his pony threw him and the fall dislodged a shower of stones and red earth to reveal part of an unsuspected temple – a most important archaeological find – Edward knew a moment of supreme happiness. He was smiling ecstatically and pressing a chunk of intricately carved sandstone to his heart when they found his body next day.

For Rosie, too, things turned out well. She soon felt the need for a more settled future than that which Captain Flashforth offered. She had been glad to stay on with him for a while, in a wing of the Maharaja's palace which had been placed at his disposal. The ladies had been furious when she refused to accompany them back to Azampur. They had imagined her services on the journey would have been well worth the slight risk that she would chatter indiscreetly upon arrival at the cantonments. But Rosie was adamant. She was staying where she was, thank you, she said . . . Thank you for nothing, you Bible-banging lot of hypocrites, she said to herself, watching the cavalcade trot out from the palace courtyard and head east, to Azampur.

So, after a short interlude with the Captain, who drank too much claret and was then inclined to show a very nasty streak of jealousy where Snuggles was concerned, Rosie thought it wiser to move on. It was better to be her own mistress, better by far. On her arrival in Bombay she found that the jewels realized a considerable fortune and no awkward questions were asked by the merchants in the silver-bazaar where she sold them among private dealers who crouched in the back of the shop, peering and weighing and bargaining – but never questioning, even though they were aware the woman in the burqa was not a Muslim – not a memsahib either . . . A Ferenghi, anyhow, they said. Shrugging, they offered her fair prices, for the haul was sumptuous. Some of the pieces looked as if they had come from royal coffers, as indeed they had.

Rosie was now a woman of independent means. She thought perhaps it would be more prudent to leave India for a while, although she had no intention of returning to the West. She took passage on a boat sailing for Alexandria, travelling as a widow whose husband, a wine importer in Delhi, had perished in the Mutiny. The ship's captain was all solicitude, 'turning the ship upside down', as the disgruntled crew said, so that Rosie and Snuggles could be more comfortable. But Rosie had done with Western men as well as Western life and the captain's solicitude got him nowhere.

Rosie always knew her own mind and always acted quickly. Soon she had set up as proprietor of an establishment similar to that kept by old Mother Baghmati in the Randi Bazaar. It was a success from the start. Her house was in a good quarter above the harbour. Her girls were the most pleasing; her dancers and musicians the best in the city; and her rosewater, arak, hookahs, betel nut and aphrodisiac draughts of the finest quality. Besides, Rosie herself was something of a novelty to the jaded Orientals, among them numbers of Indians who found its flavour markedly Hindu. This Madam was no whoremonger, or RandiBaz, as they called the customary old bawds. Rosie was as young and pretty and sometimes, they found, as willing as her girls.

It was an easy, agreeable life. She enjoyed it with that frank, childish appetite that was so irresistible to her admirers. She had devised a roof garden for Snuggles, for the house was in the city, without land, and she did not care to risk her pet's safety in the courtyard giving on to the street. So she planted tubs with oleander and orange and sweet-smelling jasmine and the green basil beloved of the East. At dusk she would sit there, cross-legged on her cushions and puffing at the hookah she had learned to savour. She would look out over the harbour where the lights were springing up along the waterfront, and the evening breeze was redolent of cloves and coffee and rancid oil. She would remember, with a sort of gentle evening melancholy, the Rao and the silver swing, and their hours together on another rooftop in the jungles of the Rani's island, so far away now. And then, farther still, Bogwood and the blue-curtained bed . . . Ah! there was a man for loving . . . Then she would remember William and Mr Brill and the Reverend – and her sordid childhood. A wave of pure happiness would replace her former melancholy. She was rich, she was free, she was in the East and she need never go back to England! She had escaped the servants' hall and the damp and the patronage forever.

And as if to share her happiness, Snuggles would run to her, squeaking and scrabbling to be lifted on to her lap. She would clap her hands and send one of her Nubian slaves running for another brew of coffee, and bamboo shoots for Snuggles. If she had known of the inscription running round the walls of the Diwan-i-Khaus, in Delhi's Red Fort, she might have echoed the Great Mogul's words: 'If there be Paradise on Earth it is this – it is this – it is this!'

But soon her paradise was threatened, for it became increasingly apparent that the bamboo rat did not thrive in this new life. Day by day he grew thinner. There was no doubt he pined for the jungles and the freedom of the island. He lay listlessly, his coat matted, his sunken flanks heaving. In vain Rosie sent out for vegetation that resembled the jungle diet he missed. She tried him on goat's milk and brandy and fresh snails . . . but to no avail, he was plainly in a decline. City life was killing him.

When Rosie realized this, she knew there was not a moment to be lost. Within a few weeks she had sold the major shares in her establishment at a solid profit and found herself a husband who lived outside the city. He was a wealthy middle-aged Arab, originally from Jeddah, who owned extensive apricot farms, (with a most remunerative sideline in pearls and hashish and more besides). He lived in feudal style in a large white house surrounded by gardens and shaded by tall trees. Beyond, stretched expanses of apricot orchards and fields of mauve opium poppies.

It was just the sort of place to suit Snuggles, thought Rosie. And so it proved to be. In no time at all he was his old self again, trotting about, snuffling at the grass and rooting under the trees. So even this threatened tragedy had turned out for the best, since it had persuaded Rosie to abandon a rather unstable single life in favour of matrimony.

Abdul ibn Zebid was a dignified, handsome figure who was never tired of praising Allah's bounty for sending him such an agreeable wife. He was a widower and Rosie being, he understood, the widow of a wealthy English nobleman, a big-game hunter, 'a nine tiger man' who had died mauled by a tiger, it was all very suitable. Abdul proved a doting, indulgent husband. Moreover, unlike so many Oriental men, he greatly appreciated both Snuggles and his wife's business abilities. He rarely went into Alexandria himself since there was a little trouble there with the authorities over some of his hashish concessions, he said. However, he quite understood that Rosie, being an English lady, was accustomed to freedoms unknown to Eastern women. And then, she had to keep an eye on the hotel in which she still held a controlling interest. As she explained, in that sort of business, the personal touch was everything. Without being rapacious, Abdul knew it was never amiss to have several irons in the fire. Between them, he and Rosie now controlled enterprises which covered most of humanity's requirements. It seemed unlikely they would ever be in straitened circumstances, which was a gratifying thought.

And here we must leave this harmonious household, as the sun sinks behind the apricot trees and the muezzin sounds from a neighbouring mosque. Snuggles is rolling rapturously in the long grass. He is quite recovered and very much petted by the slaves, to whom he is known as 'Little Disturber of Hearts'. Their master sits beneath a giant plane tree beside the stream which waters his land. He is weighing out a handful of pink pearls which his Arabian divers have just brought in. It is a fine catch and he is in a particularly benign mood. Rosie seats herself in the smart little carriage that will take her into Alexandria for a number of errands in and about the bazaars. Like every good Muslim wife, she wears her burqa.

Abdul ibn Zebid watches her admiringly. He is grateful. How happy she has made him. How well she runs his house. How ably she furthers his business interests. Truly a pearl among women! He strokes his beard and belches appreciatively, the amber and coral beads of his chaplet click through his fingers as he murmurs his prayers. In particular he praises Allah's bounty for causing the tiger to maul Rosie's late husband, (on whom be peace!), thus enabling Rosie to become his own beloved wife. Truly the ways of Fate are passing strange . . . No, it is wiser not to let her know the exact nature of his trouble with the *douane*. She could not be expected to understand about white slave traffic . . . after all, she is an English lady.

Rosie leans out of the carriage to wave, one henna-tipped, richly ringed hand emerging from the all-enveloping folds of the burqa. Her green eyes glint through the eyepieces with their usual liveliness.

'Don't wait supper for me, my love!' she calls fondly. 'I may be kept late, I have a lot of things to do this evening.'

About the Author

Lesley Blanch was a cult literary figure who influenced and inspired generations of writers, readers and critics. Her lifelong passion was for Russia, the Balkans and the Middle East. At heart a nomad, she spent the greater part of her life travelling about those remote areas her books record so vividly.

Born in London in 1904, Blanch's first career was as a book illustrator and caricaturist, and scenic and costume designer for the theatre, before turning to writing. While her reputation now rests primarily on four works of non-fiction – *The Wilder Shores of Love*, *Journey into the Mind's Eye* and *The Sabres of Paradise* and *Pierre Loti* – her early journalism brings to life the artistic melting pot that was London between the wars, and her books, something of the Middle East as it once was, before conflict and turmoil became the essence of relations between the Arab World and the West.

She left England in 1946, never to return, except as a visitor. Her marriage to Romain Gary, the French novelist and diplomat, afforded her many years of happy wanderings. After their divorce, in 1963, Blanch was seldom at her Paris home longer than to repack.

Blanch was well ahead of her time and prescient in the way she attempted to bridge West and East – especially the West and Islam.

Blanch was modern and free, with tremendous wit and style; and a traveller who took risks and relished writing about her adventures. Her life reads like a novel and sets her apart as being a true original. She died in Menton in the South of France, age 103.

Her posthumous memoirs *On the Wilder Shores of Love: A Bohemian Life* are published by Virago.

www.lesleyblanch.com

Books by Lesley Blanch

THE WILDER SHORES OF LOVE
The Stories of four ninteenth-century women who
followed the beckoning Eastern star

THE SABRES OF PARADISE
Conquest and Vengeance in the Caucasus

PIERRE LOTI
Portrait of an Escapist

PAVILIONS OF THE HEART
The Four Walls of Love

THE NINE TIGER MAN
A Satirical Romance

JOURNEY INTO THE MIND'S EYE
Fragments of an Autobiography

ON THE WILDER SHORES OF LOVE
A Bohemian Life

Printed in Great Britain
by Amazon